Ozark Tales

Of Ghosts, Spirits, Hauntings, and Monsters

Ozark Tales of Ghosts, Spirits, Hauntings and Monsters

Copyright © W. C. Jameson, 2007

Second Edition, Goldminds Publishing, LLC 2015

ISBN: 1-930584-11-3
ISBN 13: 978-1-930584-11-2

Printed in the United States of America

Without limiting the rights under the copyright reserved above, no part of this publication may be reproduced, stored in or introduced into a retrieval system, or transmitted, in any form or by any means (electronic, mechanical, photocopying, recording or otherwise), without the prior written permission of both the copyright owner and the above publisher of this book.

Goldminds Publishing
1050 Glenbrook Way, Suite 480
Hendersonville, TN 37075
www.goldmindspub.com

Ozark Tales

Of Ghosts, Spirits, Hauntings, and Monsters

By W. C. Jameson

NASHVILLE

Table of Contents

1   Introduction

7   **Ghost Lights**
9   The Joplin Ghost Light
15   The Miami Ghost Light
19   The Harrison Ghost Light
23   The Lost Slave Light of Stone County
29   The Laura Tinsley Ghost Light
35   The Mallett Town Cemetery Ghost Light

43   **Haunted Houses and Buildings**
45   The Haunted Bedroom
53   The Haunted Room
59   Taney County Haunting
65   Harding University's Mysterious Ghost
69   The Widow's Rocking Chair
73   The Haunted Cabin
79   Oklahoma Ozarks Haunted House
83   Satan's House
87   Ghost House of the Ozarks

95   **Haunted Countrysides**
97   Old Raw Head and Bloody Bones
103   The Ghost of Crooked Creek
107   The Ghost of Petit Jean
113   The Ghost of the Rebel Sentinel
117   Mount Holly Cemetery Ghost
121   The Ghosts of Happy Bend
127   The Haunted Headstone
131   Ghost Plane near Berryville
135   The Hardin Hill Haunting
139   Alf Bolin's Ghost
145   The Haunted Grave

151   **Animal Ghosts**
153   The Ghost Dog of Marion County
157   Phantom Black Panther Haunts Faulkner County

161	The Ghost Wolf
165	Oklahoma's Satan Wolf
171	Ghost Horse of Benton County
175	**Monsters**
177	The Devil in Pope County
183	The White River Monster
193	The Water Panther
197	The Lake Conway Monster
203	The Little People
207	The Creature with No Face
213	The Buffalo River Monster

Introduction

Ghosts! Spirits! Hauntings! Monsters!

Who has not thrilled to spellbinding tales of the supernatural, the unexplainable, and the mysterious? Who of us has never sat and listened in rapt wonder and awe at stories of monsters and ghosts? Who of us has not been amazed, captivated, and perhaps even terrified by such tales?

There is something about tales of ghosts, spirits, hauntings, and monsters that has fascinated and entranced human beings for centuries, something that cuts across all ages, something that stirs feelings of dread, and perhaps not a little fear in young and old alike. These stories have a way of seizing the listener, sometimes lulling, sometimes surprising them with delicious terror!

Not only have stories of ghosts and monsters been known throughout human history, tales of the unknown also cut across cultural lines. Such stories have been associated with virtually every civilization found throughout the world, and they comprise important elements of the folklore of Norse, Greek, Russian, African, East Asian, Middle Eastern, Aboriginal, American Indian, and European cultures.

The best of these tales have been told and retold to appreciative listeners, and handed down over the generations, over the centuries, via the oral tradition. During the early phases of the evolution of human society, such tales were related around campfires, in caves, and in the fields. In recent years, some of the best places to hear such tales have been in summer camp, deer camp, drawing rooms, and those occasions when relatives and friends get together.

Tales of ghosts, spirits, hauntings, and monsters have been collected from all fifty of the United States as well as a variety of geographic regions around the world and published in numerous books and journals. In virtually every case, several different cultures and ethnic groups have provided and contributed to these stories, with each group adding nuances and flavors to such tales. Many such stories have even become associated with specific countries and cultural groups.

A rich harvest of tales of ghosts, spirits, hauntings, and monsters have come from the Ozark Mountain region of the United States. Variety is apparent and, in part, is the likely result of the eclectic ethnic mix of immigrants who moved into and settled the region during the past two hundred years.

The Ozark Mountains, an extensive limestone plateau that spans portions of Arkansas, Missouri, Oklahoma, and a small part of southeastern Kansas, was originally formed from marine sediments when this region was covered by a deep ocean many millions of years ago. Following the passage of eons, the thick beds of fossil-rich limestone were uplifted and exposed to the sculpting and modifying effects of a number of erosive elements, with flowing water predominating. As the swiftly flowing streams sped down the slopes on their way to the sea, they transported grains of eroded silica and other materials, coarse sediment that further enhanced erosion as a result of their abrasive action and ultimately responsible for removing uncountable tons of rock over time. Millions of years of this type of erosion resulted in the intensive dissection of the plateau into dozens of steep-walled valleys and a great series of ridges. The ridges and crests of limestone reach toward the sky and the sunlight, but the deep and narrow valleys, called hollows, or "hollers," by the long-time residents, are sometimes characterized as dark, sometimes mysterious, and occasionally forbidding.

Joining the native Indian tribes that inhabited the Ozark Mountains were early settlers that included Upland South Anglos from Kentucky, West Virginia, Tennessee, western North and South Carolina, and northern Alabama and Georgia. In addition, some Lowland South Anglos from Mississippi as well as Southern Alabama and Georgia and the eastern Carolinas made their way into the Ozarks and established farms and communities. Brought in as slaves, Blacks were also important members of the growing population of the Ozark Mountain region, contributing not only labor but music and an incredible variety of folktales. In time, enclaves of Germans, Swiss, and Italians also evolved.

For the most part, these early Ozarkers, though eager and adventurous, were poor and uneducated. They toiled long days in the fields and woods, planted and harvested corn and other crops, hunted for game, and ran trap lines in order to provide food for the table. Diversions were few and far between for them. Church, of course, offered opportunities for communal gatherings, singing, and praying, but entertainment, as we know it today, was limited.

Entertainment for many of these early settlers came in the form of gatherings on the front porch, in the yard under a shade tree, or around the hearth during the cold weather. These gatherings often resulted in the singing of the old folk songs, playing music on stringed instruments, and, of course, story telling.

A common talent associated with a lot of early Ozarkers was the ability to tell stories. Many a late evening, following the daily plowing, harvesting, milking, wood-splitting, hay-hauling, and other chores, family members gathered to listen to stories told by relatives, sometimes several of them taking turns. Summers found them clustered on the open porch taking advantage of whatever breeze might be blowing. During the winter months when the temperatures dropped and the cold winds howled outside, they pressed close to the warmth of the fireplace as a father or a favorite uncle related tales of yore.

The topics varied, with stories ranging from the biblically inspired to those handed down from a previous generation to what happened during a shopping trip to town the previous week.

Many of these stories dealt with the mysterious and the unknown—frightening tales about ghosts, spirits, hauntings, and monsters.

These days, the grand cultural diversity encountered in the Ozark Mountains continues as more and more folk arrive to take advantage of employment, recreational, and entertainment opportunities. The addition of each new cultural group yields contributions to the regional history and lore.

The tales of ghosts, spirits, hauntings, and monsters that follow are the result of an ongoing collection and research process that has spanned three decades. On first arriving in the Ozark Mountains, I became enthralled at the abundance of lore and legend, some of which had been collected, but much of which was not. Folktales, observations, anecdotes, and folk wisdom were communicated orally by the gentle and colorful folk who inhabited these picturesque and rugged hills and lowlands. The folklorists, the historians, and sometimes merely the curious often poised nearby, eager to record the bits and pieces of this fascinating culture.

I set about gathering many of these observations and tales from the natives—information pertaining to folk medicine, the weather, gardening and farming, family, outlaws, tales of lost mines and buried treasures, feuds, death, and superstitions. I also listened to tale after tale of ghosts, spirits, hauntings, and monsters.

Many of these stories were learned as a result of sitting on the front porches of Ozark residents, listening intently while the ghostly yarns were spun. On other occasions, farmers related tales as they worked in the field and mothers spun stories as they went about the business of preparing dinner. I heard tales from people who lived in shotgun houses and from folks who lived in mansions. I have listened to the tales in churches, in taverns, and on wooden benches in front of hardware stores. From the highest ridges of the Ozark Mountains to the deepest and darkest hollows and back, the stories brimmed full with Ozark flavors and textures, tales that begged to be collected, recorded, retold, and shared.

During the course of writing a weekly newspaper column on things Ozarkan, I occasionally related a regional ghost or monster tale encountered during one of my travels. In the days that followed the appearance of such columns, letters would arrive from readers offering insight, interpretations, and versions of the tale. A number of readers also mailed in additional stories of haunted houses, stories of monsters lurking in the woods and the streams, and unexplainable and mysterious events known to have occurred in the Ozark past. In this manner I added to my own collection.

Today, these same sources remain a vital base for research and collection. In addition, expert renditions of tales of ghosts, spirits, hauntings, and monsters can now be heard at many of the growing number of storytelling conferences that are springing up around the country. Several such conferences are now held on a regular basis in the Ozarks, and offer fine examples of local lore.

In the pages that follow, the reader will encounter some of the best of these tales, tales of ghosts, spirits, hauntings, and monsters.

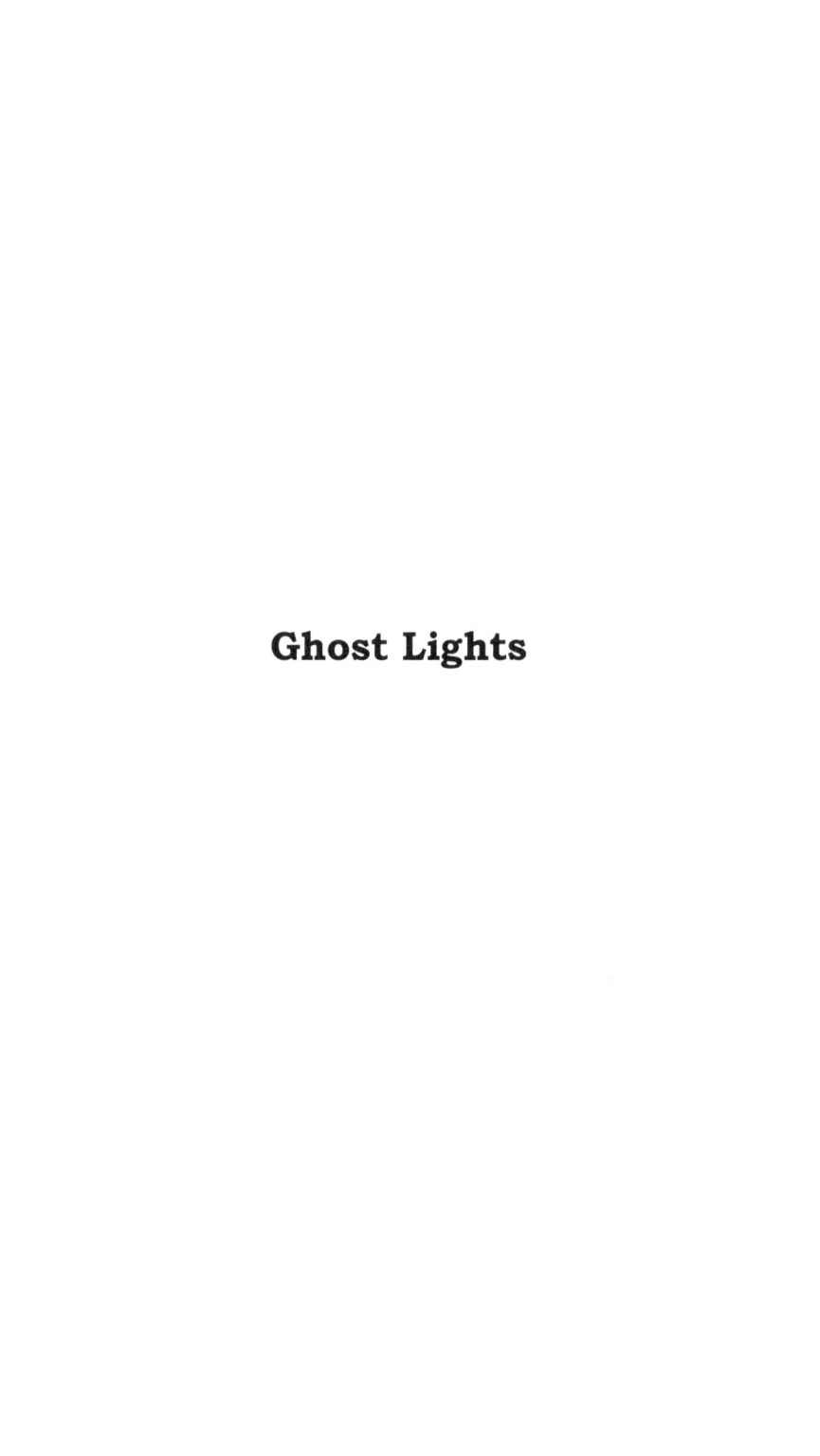

Ghost Lights

The Joplin Ghost Light

Joplin is a friendly town of some 40,000 souls located in southwestern Missouri not far from the northwestern edge of the Ozark Mountains in a region the locals refer to as the Springfield Plateau.

Well over a century ago, early settlers in that region reported what they described as a "ghostly light" emanating from an area about ten miles southwest of Joplin. The light, seen by hundreds during that time, was described as a pulsating glow that moved through the woods from tree to tree, sometimes slowly, sometimes rapidly. According to the tales told around Joplin, the light was believed to be associated with the ghost of a young Quapaw Indian brave who was searching for a loved one who had died tragically.

Over time, this strange, unearthly light was named the Joplin Ghost Light, and today it can still be seen on dark, moonless nights. If some of those who claim to see the mysterious light are to be believed, it continues to terrify.

* * *

Initially, most of the settlers who moved into southwestern Missouri during the 1880s dismissed the stories of the ghost light and attributed the phenomena to other things such as reflection and overactive imagination. Over time, however, the light persisted and frightened people so often and so badly that many of them moved out of the area, never to return.

Today, the tiny settlement of Hornet lies close to the woods where the ghost light often appears, and residents still report its occasional appearance. Some who live nearby calmly accept the light as part of Ozark lore and legend, but others confess to being frightened by it and admit to believing that something evil may reside there. Some are convinced that to even talk about it will cause bad luck to follow.

The town of Seneca lies about twenty miles southwest of Joplin, not far from Hornet, and close to the ghost light sightings. Among the earliest residents of this section of the Ozark Mountains were the Quapaw Indians who initially arrived to take advantage of the abundance of wild game and the rather agreeable climate found there. Over the years, the Quapaw hunted and trapped game, fished the streams, and coaxed crops of corn and squash from the thin soils of the hillsides and bottomlands.

Many years ago when construction work was being undertaken on what eventually became Highway 60, a number of the road workers reported seeing the ghost light. Most of the time it was spotted some distance away in the woods around dusk as they were preparing to quit for the day. The workers paused long enough to observe the light moving and flitting between trees, commenting on its eerie glow and trying to guess what it was. A few tried to chase it, but the strange light disappeared when they came close. Several of the workers said they were so spooked by the strange light that they refused to work on that particular portion of the road.

Though investigators are unsure about the possible connection, a number of local residents are convinced that an ancient Quapaw Indian graveyard that was accidentally disturbed during some of the road construction work is related to the ghost light activity. The light, claim those who have viewed it, was seen most often hovering over the old Indian burial ground.

Sometimes, according to observers, more than one light appears. During the 1940s and 1950s, the curious would drive from Joplin to the site of the old Quapaw Indian graveyard, arriving around dark to watch the lights.

Most of the time only one light was seen. It has been alternately described as white, yellow, orange, and bright red. Some say it pulsates, others claim it doesn't. Some say the light is very bright, and others have reported only a faint glow. Some have stated the light was the size of a basketball; others have identified it as being as large as a medicine ball. Most say it moves very slowly, but others state it travels in quick, jerky starts and stops, often zigzagging across the graveyard, flitting from tree to tree.

Sometimes as many as three and four lights have appeared at the same time, moving at times independently of one another, and at other times in strict precision.

One evening just past sundown, according to a woman who has been asked to tell her story many times, she and a friend arrived at the road that passed by the graveyard. They pulled to a stop, turned the lights off, and waited. As the two conversed inside the car, they were suddenly startled by a bright, white light that materialized out of the graveyard and approached the automobile from behind at a slow rate of speed.

The woman described the light as ball-shaped and beautiful with blue fingers of flame radiating from the edge. It made no sound whatsoever. When the light was within a few inches of the rear of the vehicle, it paused for a brief moment, then split in two, each half passing on either side of the car! Then, astonishingly, the two halves met at the front of the car, rejoined into one, and proceeded down the middle of the road until it was out of sight. The woman and her friend were frightened into speechlessness and remained in the car, unmoving, for several minutes. Later, the woman stated that when the light passed by the sides of the car, she was so scared that she could actually hear the sound of her own heart beating.

Many people who have seen and studied the Joplin Ghost Lights claim they are the spirits of the dead who are interred in the old Indian graveyard. One of the most accepted tales of the origin of this mysterious light, however, has to do with lost love.

According to an old Quapaw legend, the light is the ghost of a young Indian, a promising warrior and hunter who would someday be a leader of his tribe. He was betrothed to a beautiful Quapaw maiden, and together the two made plans for their marriage, a home, and children. For reasons that remain unclear, the young woman's father promised her to another brave, a member of a neighboring tribe. Heartbroken, she decided to commit suicide rather than be married to someone she did not love. One day while the young warrior she loved was away on a hunting trip, she leaped off a tall bluff, her body landing on a jumble of rocks below. She was found later that same day and secretly buried by her father somewhere in the tribal burial ground located near Hornet.

Several days later when the brave returned to the camp, he was informed of her death. He searched far and wide for her grave site but was never able to find it.

For the rest of his life, the Indian looked for the grave of his loved one. At night, he fashioned a torch and roamed the cemetery, always hoping to find the place where she was laid to rest.

Though this story is the one most widely accepted by those who live in the region, it does not explain the appearance of multiple lights.

Today, people still come to the region of the old Quapaw burial ground near Hornet to observe what is still called the Joplin Ghost Light. Over the years, experts who study ghost light phenomena have arrived to study and describe the glow. They always come away with no explanation. Whatever the origin, this strange light continues to remain a mystery today.

The Miami Ghost Light

Miami, Oklahoma, is located in the extreme northeastern corner of the Sooner State in Ottawa County. It is set among the picturesque rolling foothills of the Ozark Mountains where pasture and woods dominate the landscape.

On certain dark, misty, foggy nights a strange light appears out in the middle of one of the pastures not far from Miami, a light that sways back and forth as it moves along approximately two to three feet above the ground. The light can be observed for several minutes at a time until it finally disappears around a grove of trees or simply vanishes.

Called the Miami Ghost Light by area residents, this strange glow is all that remains of a very sad story.

* *
*

Late one winter evening during the 1930s, a widow, peering through the dense fog that covered her pasture, observed that her three cows had gotten out. On closer inspection, she noticed that a portion of the rail fence had been knocked down and the cattle had walked through the opening.

Returning to the house, the widow lit a lantern, handed it to her fourteen year-old daughter, and sent her out into the dark, dreary night to herd the livestock back into the field and fix the fence.

The widow bundled the daughter up into sweater, coat, gloves, and shawl, and waved goodbye to her as the young girl stepped off of the rough-hewn plank front porch. The widow watched as the girl's form and the swinging lantern was gradually engulfed by the dense, swirling fog. Little could she have known that it was the last time she would ever see her daughter.

After an hour passed and the cattle had not been returned to the field, the widow began to grow concerned. Another hour went by, and the girl had still not returned. Three hours later, the widow, now frantic, left the house in search of her daughter.

The widow was still searching at sunrise, but could find no trace of the girl. When the morning sun had finally burned away the fog, she ran to a neighbor's house and explained what had happened. The neighbor, enlisting the help of other families living nearby, undertook a systematic search for the young girl that lasted for several days and covered the woods and the fields for several miles around.

She was never found.

The lost cattle were eventually located and returned to the pasture, and though an occasional search for the missing girl was conducted during the following days, no sign of her ever turned up.

Each night for the rest of her life, the widow left the house after sundown and, carrying a lantern, roamed the pastures, fields, and forests in search of her lost daughter. From time to time she would pause in her search, raise the lantern high above her head, and call out her daughter's name.

As the years passed, the old widow grew insane from grief. Several attempts were made to place her in the care of an institution, but she refused, insisting she needed to continue the search for her missing daughter.

Eventually the old woman died and was buried in a nearby cemetery. She passed away one October, about the time the color of the Ozark foliage turned from green to orange and red.

Three months following the burial of the old widow, a winter storm struck the area. Temperatures dropped, the skies turned grey, rain and snow fell for two days, and a dense fog enshrouded the hills and valleys.

Melvin Williams was a cattle farmer who lived in the area during that time. Late one evening while he was out checking his livestock, Williams noticed a moving light several hundred yards away in the old widow's pasture. The light appeared to come from a swinging lantern, and was traveling slowly across the field as though someone were looking for something.

Curious, Williams crossed his field, climbed a fence, and entered the widow's pasture. He kept his eye on the moving light the entire time, and watched as it entered a nearby grove of trees. Williams finally came within a few feet of the strange light, and what he saw caused him to freeze with terror. The glow, similar to one that might come from a kerosene lantern, hovered about two-and-a-half feet above the ground, swinging back and forth, but no one was holding it!

Williams watched the pulsating glow for about thirty seconds when it suddenly disappeared. Shaken, he returned to his house and told his wife what he had seen.

Within a few days, nearly everyone in the community had heard the story of Melvin Williams' encounter with the mysterious ghost light. Several neighbors began arriving at the Williams farm each night to see if they could also view the strange glow in the distance.

They were not disappointed. Night after night for three weeks, onlookers, sometimes numbering as many as fifteen at a time, watched as a swinging, lantern-like glow slowly crossed the late widow's pasture and disappeared into a grove of trees. From that time on, the ghost light was seen occasionally, but always on dark, foggy nights.

Over time, the residents of this part of northeastern Oklahoma came to the conclusion that the strange glow came from a lantern carried by the ghost of the old widow, a ghost that somehow returned from the grave to continue the search for the lost daughter.

The Harrison Ghost Light

Some old-time Harrison, Arkansas, residents tell a story of a mysterious ghost light that has been seen for well over a century, a light that appears at a second floor window of an old Civil War-era home.

The current occupants of the rural Boone County house, it is said, have seen the light on numerous occasions. While they were initially frightened by the spectacle, and are still often surprised by it, they have never been harmed by the mysterious presence.

* * *

The story surrounding the ghost light has its origins in the War Between the States. While serving in a fighting unit in Tennessee, a young Confederate soldier from Bear Springs, Arkansas, located a few miles northwest of Harrison, received a message that his family's homestead had been attacked by some raiders who killed his mother and father. Frantic and consumed with grief and worry, he requested permission to return home. When his request was refused, he simply deserted his infantry company one night and walked the entire distance from Tennessee to northwestern Arkansas.

The two-story frame house had once been impressive, and was one of only a few of its type that existed in this area at the time. The house was built by the young soldier's father and uncles and was considered quite distinctive with dormer-style windows and an exquisitely hand-carved wooden front door. An expansive covered porch extended well into the front yard and provided a setting for gatherings and visits.

It was a moonless night when the exhausted soldier, after weeks of traveling, arrived at the home where he was born and raised. He entered the dark, quiet structure, lit a lantern, and began to search about. He found nothing amiss until he reached his parents' bedroom, a second floor room facing the road. There, splattered across the hardwood floor, were dried bloodstains.

Realizing at once that his mother and father had indeed been killed, the soldier, filled with grief and still holding the lantern, pulled a knife from his belt scabbard, raised it high above his head, and then plunged it deep into his own heart.

Late one evening the following week, a neighbor chanced to be passing by the house. Glancing up at one of the dormer windows, he spotted what he described as the dim glow of a lantern, suggesting that someone was moving about inside. The neighbor had heard about the killings and knew there should be no one in the house. Cautiously, he entered the structure, listening carefully for sounds of a prowler on the second floor but hearing nothing. When the neighbor finally climbed the stairs and entered the bedroom, he found the body of the dead soldier, a knife sticking out of his chest. Lying nearby was a lantern, unlit. When the neighbor placed a hand on the lantern, he found it cold, indicating it had not burned in several days and therefore could not have been the source of the light he had seen from the road. Believing that the room to be haunted, the neighbor fled from the house and immediately reported the incident to authorities.

Three months later, another neighbor, along with his young wife, was returning by wagon along the road to their home around midnight when they happened to pass by the two-story house. Distracted by something in the window, the neighbor turned in his seat to see a pulsating glow as if from a dying lantern. Recalling that the house had been empty for some time, he stopped the wagon, pulled his rifle from the beneath the seat, and told his wife he was going to investigate.

After crossing the overgrown front yard, the neighbor opened the unlocked door to the house and peered in. All was dark and quiet, but just enough light from the moon allowed him to see inside. Slowly, he inched his way into the large room, moved toward the stairs, and began climbing toward the second floor. After what seemed like an eternity, the neighbor arrived at the door of the room from which the light had shone. Wary, he stepped into the room, rifle at the ready. He was greeted only by an eerie silence and a darkness broken slightly by the dim light of the half moon shining in the window. Calling out, he received no response. Glancing down at the floor, the neighbor could see the blood-splattered floor in the moon's light. What frightened him the most was that the blood appeared to be fresh. Bending over, he touched the tip of a finger to the blood and found it damp and wet. He left the house quickly, climbed into the wagon, and sped away.

Though numerous attempts have been made to remove the bloodstains from the second-floor room, they have all been unsuccessful. During the 1970s, the floor was stripped down to the bare wood by a commercial floor finishing company. When this was done, a brand new coat of fresh varnish was spread evenly throughout the room, leaving it clear and shiny. When the finisher had completed the job, several people examined the floor and no evidence of the stain was apparent. One week later, however, the bloodstains reappeared at the exact same place, and when initially discovered, it was wet and sticky.

Additional attempts were made to remove the bloodstains, and all of them failed. Resigned to the fact that it was fruitless, the current occupants of the house have covered them over with a rug. The door to the room is kept locked and no one is allowed inside except to clean.

The Harrison Ghost Light, as it has come to be called, is still seen from time to time by people who travel down the seldom-used road that passes in front of the old house. It is always seen in the same window, always around midnight, on cloudy nights as well as clear.

The Lost Slave Light of Stone County

Not many people are aware that slaves were quite common in the Ozark Mountains for several decades during the period before the Civil War. Many early settlers acquired extensive land holdings there, converted hundreds of acres of forest into pasture for livestock and a lot of bottomland into corn fields. Slaves were considered necessary to handle all the work required to maintain such a large enterprise, and in the years prior to the Civil War many moved into the region along with their white owners. The ghost light of one such slave still appears today along the crest of Cow Mountain in Arkansas' Stone County.

* * *

Farm work was extremely difficult in the Ozarks: The thin, poor soils often yielded meager harvests and provided very little nutrient for the grass that was eagerly consumed by hungry cattle. Additionally, the slaves worked long hours and often stayed up all night long guarding livestock from predatory wild animals, Indians, and white rustlers.

Over the years, small groups of slaves from different farms often associated with one another. Strong bonds were formed, and occasionally the workers from the area farms would gather together during certain times of the year for celebrations and festivities. During these occasions, relationships were struck and strengthened from their mutual hardships. The young men of one farm often met young women from another, and marriages were consummated.

In the western part of Stone County during the 1840s, one successful farmer boasted ownership of some twenty-five slaves, all of whom lived in shanties along the north-facing slope of Cow Mountain near the present-day town of Mountain View. On the southern side of the mountain lived another group of slaves owned by a neighboring land owner.

The mountain, rising a bit over five hundred feet from the adjacent lowlands, was an east-west oriented limestone structure stretching for about a mile and a half. As with most of the Ozark Mountains, Cow Mountain had been uplifted millions of years ago. Ages of subsequent erosion from flowing water carved into the soft limestone rock, forming deep canyons and adjacent valleys.

On several occasions, the land owners on each side of the mountain attempted to plant crops on the hillsides, but because the soil was so thin and prone to wash away down the steep slopes during periods of heavy rain, they eventually gave up. Instead, they left the mountain in timber which they used for firewood, log cabins, barns, sheds, smokehouses, and bridge materials.

From time to time members of the two slave communities on the north and south slopes of Cow Mountain gathered together for celebrations, Sunday church services, and other special events. Since the distance around the mountain was so great, they often climbed the steep path that switchbacked up the slope to the top of the ridge and then down the other side.

One spring there was great feasting and revelry when the daughter of Ephraim Williams, the black patriarch of the north slope slaves, married a young man from the south slope. The newlyweds were well-liked by both the blacks and whites, and even the owners of the two plantations, along with their families, attended the wedding ceremony. At the conclusion of the festivities, arrangements were made with the owners and the couple went to live in the south slope community.

Approximately nine months later, Ephraim Williams received word late one night that his daughter was about to give birth to her first child. Wishing to be by her side when his new grandchild arrived, Ephraim awakened his wife and told her he was going to climb the mountain and cross over to the other side to the south slope community. He said he would return with the news about their grandchild as soon as possible.

The night air was dense with fog as Williams' wife, along with several other slaves who had awakened, stood in the paths that wound between and among the shanties to cheer Ephraim's departure. The old man lit a lantern and, carrying it in his right hand, kissed his wife, waved goodbye to his neighbors, and proceeded along the steep path that wound up the mountainside through the forest.

As Ephraim walked away, he turned occasionally to wave to the small group that had gathered. Eventually, he disappeared into the fog and woods. For several minutes, the slaves watched as the glare of the lantern light receded into the forest.

For almost an hour they stood in the darkness and visited with one another. Presently, one of them pointed up toward the crest of the mountain, drawing everyone's attention to the bobbing lantern that made its way along that portion of the trail where the forest was thin and the trees spaced far apart. Soon, even the bright glare of the lantern disappeared into the growing mist.

It was the last time anyone ever saw Ephraim Williams.

When the dawn of the following morning finally burned off the fog, several north slope slaves gathered at the end of the trail to await the return of Ephraim. Around noon, they spotted someone walking down the path. A shout rang out in the small community announcing the impending arrival, and soon residents began gathering in anticipation of seeing Ephraim.

When the visitor was still a hundred yards in the distance, the north slope residents could see that it was not Ephraim but a resident of the south slope community. As the visitor approached the gathered slaves, he proudly announced the birth of a strong and healthy son to the happy couple.

When the north slope slaves asked of the whereabouts of Ephraim, the surprised visitor stated he had not seen him, that the old man never arrived at the village. At first puzzled, and then concerned, several of the north slope slaves, following a brief parley, headed up the trail to begin a search for their revered leader.

For several days, the ridge and slopes of the mountain were carefully searched, but Ephraim Williams was nowhere to be found. It was as though he simply vanished.

Late one night several weeks after the disappearance of Ephraim Williams, the north slope slaves were awakened by someone calling excitedly from the base of the mountain. Thinking it might be Ephraim, they ran out of their cabins to investigate. Instead, they found Ephraim's brother, Joshua, and he was pointing at something up on the ridge. There, at the crest of Cow Mountain, the slaves could see what appeared to be a lantern light moving as though carried by someone walking along the trail. Two men ran past Joshua and up the path, their intention to approach the moving light to see if it was being carried by Ephraim. Some time later when they came to within only twenty feet of the glow, it disappeared!

For the next twenty-five years, what has since come to be called the Lost Slave Light of Stone County was often seen bobbing along the crest. Most sightings occurred on foggy evenings, and the story told throughout the region credited the light as coming from the lantern carried by the ghost of Ephraim Williams, still trying to find its way across the mountain.

Today, all traces of the old slave quarters are gone from both slopes, but the mountain maintains its prominence on the landscape and continues to serve as a landmark for travelers. Even the old trail that passed from the north slope to the south can still be found.

Now and then, someone driving by on nearby State Highway 66 on a foggy night can still see the ghostly light of Ephraim Williams moving slow and deliberate along the crest of Cow Mountain.

The Laura Tinsley Ghost Light

During the decade of the 1890s, the Tinsley Farm in western Oklahoma was the home to a herd of fine cattle, a few horses, and about a dozen goats.

Herbert L. Tinsley regarded himself as a hard worker, a devoted family man, and a knowledgeable cattleman. His cattle were the pride of that part of the Ozark Mountains and he maintained a profitable and somewhat satisfying business on the side of selling horses as riding stock.

The goat herd belonged to Tinsley's young daughter, Laura. He had given her a kid as a pet two years earlier, and Laura became fascinated with the animal. She proved to be adept at caring for the goat and asked her father if she could start her own herd. He agreed, and during the next few months he added does to her herd that he acquired in trade with neighbors and customers.

Soon, Laura Tinsley was milking several goats and selling the product to nearby residents, adding a small amount of money from time to time to the family savings.

Laura's favorite goat was her first one - the one given to her by her father. She named the billy goat Henry, and took him everywhere she went—to town, for walks in the woods, and for company as she performed her chores on the farm. Henry trailed along behind the girl almost everywhere she went. He had to be penned up when she departed for school, otherwise he would have followed her there.

Tending goats was not always an easy job. Sometimes wolves and coyotes raided the goat pen. On two occasions, the wild predators killed a goat each time they attacked. Both times, Henry tried valiantly to fight off the attackers, but to no avail.

During the most recent attack, Henry's right front flank had been torn open by a wolf. Laura, her father, and her oldest brother raced from the house to the pen just in time to chase away the wolf before it could do further harm, likely saving Henry's life. Laura doctored Henry's wound and stayed up with him all night, standing guard to make certain the attack was not repeated.

As Henry grew older, he started wandering away when Laura let him out of the pen. Occasionally he found tasty vegetation in the nearby woods and headed there. Sometimes he liked to roam down by the creek and munch on the watercress that grew along the bank. Despite her almost constant attention, Henry would sometimes disappear from sight for several hours at a time before Laura could finally locate him. Eventually, she tied a bell around his neck. When the Billy goat disappeared, she would simply follow the sound of the tinkling bell until she located him and returned him to the pen.

One quiet early autumn evening following dinner and a Bible reading, Laura went out to the pen to check on her goats before going to bed. She counted them and noticed one was missing. It was Henry.

She looked all around the pen, in the nearby horse corral, and the barn, but could not find Henry. Presently, she thought she heard the sound of his bell coming from some distance away toward the west. The sound was coming from the woods, and Laura was certain Henry wandered in that direction in order to dine on some of his favorite flowers.

Laura returned to the house and told her mother and father she was going to go look for Henry. Since the sun had nearly set, her mother insisted she take a lantern with her. With her father's help, Laura lit the lantern and ran out of the house toward the woods in search of Henry.

Herb Tinsley seated himself on the front porch, lit his pipe, and relaxed from his day's chores in the darkness as he watched the lantern light bobbing away in the distance. He could hear Laura calling for Henry, her voice growing ever fainter as she entered the woods.

Now and again, Tinsley caught sight of the lantern moving through the far woods as it passed through a portion of it where the trees were thinly spaced. For almost an hour, he watched the movements of the light in the woods until it finally disappeared.

For another hour, Tinsley sat on the porch waiting for his daughter to return with Henry, but there was no sign of her. Presently, he rose and scanned the distance for some sign of the light, but he saw none. Concerned, he left the porch and walked across the field into the woods in search of her. He called over and over but never received an answer.

All night long Herb Tinsley looked for his daughter, calling her name until he was hoarse. He never found her. At sunrise, the rest of the family, along with several neighbors, joined in the search and, though they looked for the young girl the entire day, she was never found.

In fact, Laura Tinsley was never seen again, and what became of her remains a mystery to this day, one that continues to perplex those familiar with the story.

What is even more mysterious, however, is the occasional appearance of strange light moving through the woods where Laura Tinsley was last seen.

The light first appeared one autumn night about three years following Laura's disappearance. Herbert Tinsley was the first to see it, and his blood froze as he watched it bobbing and moving through the woods exactly as it did the night Laura disappeared. The first night the strange light appeared, Tinsley raced from the porch to the woods, thinking somehow he was going to see his daughter returning from looking for her lost goat. He came to within thirty feet of the light, he later stated, when it suddenly disappeared.

Each year at the same time, the light appeared and remained visible for several evenings before vanishing, and each year, Herbert Tinsley watched it and thought of his beautiful daughter whom he missed so much.

Ten years after the disappearance of Laura Tinsley, Herbert passed away. The farm was sold shortly thereafter and the surviving family members moved to California.

The old Tinsley farm, located near the present-day town of Proctor in Adair County, has had a succession of owners since then. Each of the residents has reported seeing the ghost light.

As recently as the early 1990s, visitors to the region from the nearby cities of Tahlequah, Oklahoma, and Fayetteville, Arkansas, have reported observing the ghost light during the first two weeks of October.

Experts in physics and mysterious lights who have heard about the case of Laura Tinsley have also visited the site and have offered a variety of explanations, invoking the supposed role of below-ground quartz deposits, underground energies, fault lines, and the activity of surface gases. While residents of the area patiently listen to the scientific explanations of the mysterious light, they remain convinced it is the ghost of Laura Tinsley searching for her goat.

The Mallett Town Cemetery Ghost Light

Mallett Town, Arkansas, is a tiny rural community located in Faulkner County in the southern reaches of the Ozark Mountains where the range grades toward the Arkansas River. Farming dominates the local economy here, and like most locations in this area it's good some years and not so good in others, usually as a result of the vagaries of the constantly changing local weather.

Not far from the central part of the community lies Mallett Town Bottoms, a low-lying area sandwiched between woods and agricultural fields. Walking through the Bottoms, as most area residents call it, can sometimes be an intimidating experience. To do so on a late summer afternoon is to experience a deep, windless, and oppressive heat and humidity, in spite of the fact that large trees and thick and dense vegetation shade much of the area.

Mallett Town Bottoms at night is a different experience altogether. A moist quiet pervades the single dirt road that transects the region. Passing along the road in a vehicle, the driver often spots flickering images at the periphery of his vision, images that disappear when he looks in their direction. Many who have driven this road at night have confessed to feeling a strange and blessed relief when they finally come out of it and enter the slightly busier two-lane paved road.

Those who have walked through Mallett Town Bottoms at night tell stories of strange sounds coming from the dense foliage that lines the road. Some of the sounds are identifiable as frogs and owls, but others are noises no one has ever heard before. Tales of strange creatures living in the Bottoms occasionally reach the ears of outsiders, but for the most part the residents don't talk much about them.

On the west side of Mallett Town Bottoms, where the dirt road climbs a low rise and curves its way toward the community lies the Mallett Town Cemetery, a graveyard that somehow seems too large for the small town that it serves. Surrounding the cemetery is a chain link fence, the grass growing near its base kept trimmed and neat. Close to the road can be seen some new headstones, but toward the back of the cemetery near the crest of a low ridge are found the older monuments, some of them dating back more than a century. A walk through the well-kept graveyard reveals several with dates from the 1860s and 1870s.

During one summer afternoon visit, the cemetery was quiet save for a caretaker making the rounds. Insects buzzed loudly from the adjacent forest, butterflies swooped among the gravestones, and mockingbirds and cardinals flitted through the tree canopy.

Ozark Tales 37

The cemetery at night, according to several who live in the area, is quite different, for it is haunted.

Since the 1980s, according to what limited research is available, a strange ghost light has been seen in the cemetery. The light is slightly larger than a softball, appears somewhat reddish, and is seen on moonless as well as bright moonlit nights. According to the caretaker, the light generally appears in the area of two tall, white headstones, one indicating the deceased passed away in 1923, the other in 1932. Norwood is the name on both stones.

Over the years, the light has been seen often, but those who live in this out-of-the-way area seldom comment on it, preferring to accept it as one of those strange, oftentimes unexplainable occurrences men are faced with from time to time. Outsiders are not common here, and many of the residents prefer it that way.

Occasionally, however, someone comes along with burning curiosities and a need for explanation. One such person is a cattle farmer who lived in a older brick house a little over a mile from the cemetery. The farmer was preparing to go to bed late one evening during the 1990s when he heard a knock on his front door. He opened it to find an elderly couple he knew—they appeared somewhat agitated and asked the farmer for his help. They told him they had just driven by the cemetery and thought they saw someone inside the fence among the headstones with a flashlight. They were concerned that pranksters might be turning over headstones and wanted the younger farmer to ride back with them in their truck with them to have a look.

The farmer climbed into the pick-up as the old man started the engine, and together the three rode the short distance to the cemetery. As they approached, the old man slowed a bit. As the truck negotiated the curve in the road as it rose out of the Bottoms the headlights swept across the graveyard from left to right, casting the entire lot in light. Most of the headstones were easily seen, and no prowlers appeared to be about. Pulling the truck into the short driveway that served as an entrance to the cemetery, the passengers peered out of the window, trying to find a trespasser among the monuments. There was nothing, only silence, save for the smooth idling of the truck.

After a few moments passed and the occupants of the truck were satisfied no one was in the cemetery, the driver backed up into the dirt road and pointed the truck back in the direction from which they had just come. As they pulled away down the sloping road, they looked back toward the cemetery and there, suddenly, appeared the light.

The old man slammed on the brakes and the farmer leaped out of the truck and started walking toward the cemetery. As he did, the strange light disappeared. He stood in one spot for several seconds, but the light failed to reappear. Presently, he climbed back into the pick-up and was taken home.

For several evenings thereafter, the farmer thought about the light he observed many times and wondered what could have caused it. At first he considered it might have been a reflection of the moon, but there was no moon that evening.

A few weeks later at Sunday church services, the farmer encountered the old man who drove him to the cemetery and they struck up a conversation. Soon, the talk turned toward the mysterious Mallett Town Cemetery light, and the elderly gentleman informed the farmer that he had seen the light several more times while driving down the road late at night. The conversation only served to pique the farmer's curiosity even more.

One evening after the sun had been down for a couple of hours, the farmer decided to drive to the cemetery for another look. After passing through the humidity-hazed bottoms he pulled up to the cemetery and turned off his lights. He leaned back on the seat, peering through the darkness into the cemetery, but saw nothing. He turned off his engine and settled back into the seat, listening to the noises of frogs and crickets.

Then he saw it!

The light took shape just beyond the crest of the low hill. As the farmer watched, the ghost light pulsated but remained in one position. Later, he recalled, it looked like the light from a flashlight, but it was red and there was no beam. Then, after several seconds, the light simply disappeared.

Following that night, the farmer went back to the cemetery on more than a dozen occasions and saw the ghost light on nearly every visit. He said the light sometimes appears when his headlights are off, sometimes when they are on. It is seen on bright moonlit nights as well as dark overcast nights.

From time to time, the farmer would mention the ghost light to others who lived in the area. They would sometimes admit to seeing it also, although it was apparent they were uncomfortable talking about it.

* * *

A few years after the farmer first saw the ghost light, he related the incident to a newspaper reporter. Intrigued, the journalist, finding himself not far from Mallett Town Bottoms late one night, turned off the paved road and drove toward the cemetery. The Bottoms, he recalled later, were "spooky," with sights and sounds unlike anything he had ever seen before. By the time he passed through the bottoms and was following the road up the low rise and around the curve toward the cemetery, his nerves were strained and his anticipation high.

Like the farmer, the journalist intended to park in front of the cemetery, turn off his lights, and await the appearance of the ghost light. It was not to happen that way. Before he could even slow his vehicle in preparation for his turn into the cemetery entrance, the ghost light appeared! One moment the graveyard was dark, and then the light appeared, pulsating at the exact spot the journalist expected to find it. The light stayed in sight as he braked and stared out the window, remaining in view for several seconds. Then, as suddenly as it appeared, it winked out.

In the darkness, the journalist pulled up to the fence and killed the engine. Still experiencing the surge of adrenalin from the seeing the ghost light only moments earlier, he waited and hoped for its reappearance. He stayed silent and unmoving for nearly twenty minutes, but the cemetery remained dark and quiet. Finally, believing he had seen the last of the ghost light for this evening, he started his engine and backed into the road. As he pulled away, he glanced quickly back at the cemetery and saw it again. Almost as if it was mocking him, toying with him, the ghost light glowed brightly where it was seen earlier. It seemed, he said later, that this time the light was moving as if it were following him at a distance, and appeared to be approaching at a slow but steady rate of speed.

With his skin prickling with fear and his heart pounding furiously, the journalist pushed the gas pedal to the floor and sped away, spraying gravel and dust behind him. Just before he turned the corner and entered the Bottoms, he looked in his rear view mirror and continued to see the light. He later stated he had the feeling it was laughing at him.

Numerous attempts have been made to explain the Mallett Town Cemetery ghost light, but few can agree on the cause. Some wonder what, if anything, it has to do with the two tall, white headstones the bore the name "Norwood." Old-timers in the area cannot recall any circumstance regarding the Norwoods that would cause a ghost light to appear near their resting places.

Why the ghost light only began appearing since 1980 is also a mystery. When questioned, area old-timers can recall nothing special about that year except for the fact that it was likely the time of the worst drought in the history of the Ozarks, an event that hardly seems capable of generating ghost lights.

One elderly woman, however, mentioned that a mild earthquake was felt by her and several others in the area of the cemetery in 1980. While no definitive proof has ever been found associating ghost lights with earthquakes, there seems to exist a correlation between the two at other locations. In several early studies of ghost lights, many of them were found in regions associated with active fault zones.

One researcher advanced the notion that the present cemetery at Mallett Town may be located atop an ancient Indian burial ground. At such sites, according to the researcher, there have been dozens of ghost light sightings—some individual lights and others appearing in groups of two or more. No one, however, has ever been able to provide an explanation for this strange phenomenon.

According to nearby residents, numerous Indian artifacts have been found in the area over the past several decades. Only additional research will determine if the present-day Mallett Town Cemetery is located atop an ancient Indian burial ground.

In the meantime, the Mallett Town Cemetery ghost light continues to mystify, beguile, and frighten observers.

Haunted Houses and Buildings

The Haunted Bedroom

Deep in the thick pine forests of northwestern Arkansas' Newton County can be found an old log cabin that once contained a haunted bedroom. Perhaps it still does.

Many believe the house, now long abandoned and left to ruin in the woods far from roads and trails, may still serve as the residence of the ghost of an old man who lived there many years ago. The ghost has made its presence known to several people and, while apparently harmless, continues to frighten any who would attempt to keep it locked up.

The ghost also continues to mystify.

For longer than anyone in Newton County can remember, an elderly man by the name of Tolliver lived in a decaying, crudely fashioned log house far out in the woods and miles from neighbors. No one living today can recall Tolliver's first name, and a few said the old man never gave one—he just told people to call him Tolliver.

No road reached Tolliver's dwelling, just a path barely wide enough to accommodate the mule he rode.

A somewhat reclusive sort of fellow, Tolliver rarely came into the settlements, and when he did it was to purchase coffee, sugar, candy, and tobacco.

Tolliver's flowing white hair and long beard went uncut for long periods of time and he seldom bathed, according to those who remembered him. Despite what many of the area townsfolk perceived as a rather relaxed personal hygiene regimen, Tolliver was regarded as a good-hearted, harmless, and gentle old man. He generally kept to himself and, though not particularly friendly or outgoing with most of the town's adult residents, always had a kind word for the children, sometimes offered them candy, and would tell them stories about Indians, outlaws, mountain men and trappers and living way out in the woods with all of the different animals such as wolves and bears and mountain lions.

One spring when old man Tolliver didn't show up in town for several weeks in a row, a few of the local men went to his cabin to investigate. With some difficulty, they found his house in a deep, quiet pocket of the forest, but Tolliver was nowhere to be seen. After hollering a greeting several times and receiving no answer, the men let themselves into the cabin.

In the bedroom, they found Tolliver's corpse and reckoned he had been dead for at least ten days. The body was found lying on the floor in a position suggesting that, just before he died, old man Tolliver was trying very hard to crawl out of the room. Since there were no marks on him and no signs of violence, they presumed he simply died of natural causes.

Tolliver was buried in a level plot behind his cabin under a spreading hickory tree. The grave was covered over with a layer of heavy rocks to discourage scavengers and marked with a slab of limestone that bore only the name "Tolliver" crudely chiseled onto the surface. No one knew when Tolliver was born. In fact, no one ever knew where he had come from or how long he had been living in those woods.

Several years passed, and a couple by the name of Spradlin moved into the Tolliver cabin and began raising hogs in the nearby woods. In those days, squatters often took up residence in abandoned structures. The newcomers fixed up the old dwelling, re-chinked the spaces between the weathered logs, hung new windows, reshingled the roof, and applied fresh masonry to the crude fireplace and chimney.

On hearing the story of old man Tolliver's body being found in the bedroom, the Spradlins, being somewhat superstitious, decided to sleep in another room and used the bedroom only for storage.

Late one night about two weeks after moving into the old cabin, Lon Spradlin was awakened by the squeaky sound of a doorknob turning. This sound was immediately followed by another—that of a door creaking open very slowly on ancient, rusty hinges. The sound seemed quite loud in the nighttime stillness. By this time, Lon's wife, Ruby, was awake, and together the two sat in bed, huddled closely and listening intently. At first, they thought an intruder was entering the house, so Spradlin retrieved his rifle which was leaning against the wall in a far corner of the room.

The two listened intently for several more minutes, but only silence reigned, a deep, grave-like stillness that frightened the husband and wife even more than the strange noise of the opening door. After another five minutes of what was becoming an unbearable quiet, Spradlin set aside his rifle, lit a lantern, and slowly walked through the house to investigate.

As Spradlin passed from room to room, everything appeared normal until he reached the door to the storeroom. He was certain he had closed it tight earlier in the day, but now it was sitting wide open. Peering into the storeroom, he saw nothing other than the items he had stored there—kegs and crates stacked neatly against one walls, tool arranged in one corner, harnesses, and feed for the chickens. When he closed the door this time, Spradlin made certain that it clicked shut. Two hours later, the Spradlins were suddenly awakened once again by the opening of the storeroom door!

Each night for the next two weeks, the door to the bedroom opened on its own, even after Lon Spradlin closed it repeatedly, often as many as five or six times during the same night. Finally, Spradlin attached a hook-and-eye latch to the door frame and the door, and before retiring to bed one night, shut the door tightly and latched it securely.

Sometime that night, Spradlin was awakened by the sound of the latch hook snapping open and the doorknob turning. As he and Ruby lay quietly in the bed surrounded by the darkness of this moonless night, the sound of the door slowly opening on old, rusty hinges echoed once again throughout the house. In the morning when Spradlin went to investigate, he was surprised to discover the storeroom door standing wide open once again.

The next day, Spradlin retrieved a hammer from his wagon bed and filled the bib pocket in his overalls with heavy nails. After closing the storeroom door tightly, he secured it, using at least eight of the nails. The following morning, however, the two awoke to find the door open as before, the thick nails having been pulled from the frame.

After enduring several weeks of the troubling haunting, Spradlin described the strange happenings to some of the men in town one afternoon. One old resident, after pondering his neighbor's dilemma, puffed slowly on his pipe and offered the suggestion that Tolliver's ghost might still be in the room and was attempting to get out, just as Tolliver himself was apparently trying to do when he died.

On arriving home that evening, Spradlin removed the storeroom door from the frame and set it outside. Tolliver's ghost, he reasoned, could now come and go as it pleased, hopefully without disturbing anyone.

From that time on for as long as Lon and Ruby Spradlin lived in the cabin, they were never again bothered by the ghost of old man Tolliver.

As the years passed, the Spradlins eventually abandoned the Tolliver house and moved away, some say to Texas. Untended, the cabin fell into a state of disrepair.

During the 1970s, two deer hunters chanced upon the Tolliver cabin while hiking through the area in search of game. They set up a temporary camp in the dwelling, went out each morning to hunt, and returned late each afternoon to prepare dinner. At night they slept peacefully on the plank floor. After determining that no one owned the structure, they decided to make it liveable so they could use it as a deer camp each year.

While cleaning out and fixing up the old dwelling, one of the deer hunters found an discarded door outside leaning against the back wall. He brought it inside, reattached it to the hinges from which it apparently came, and closed it tightly. Late that evening following a big meal cooked over a fire in the hearth. One of the men casually mentioned to the other that while he was looking around the yard he chanced upon a grave only a few yards from the house, a grave that bore a headstone with the name "Tolliver" carved into it. In a little while, the two men fell asleep.

Around midnight, the deer hunters suddenly jerked awake at the unmistakable sound of a door creaking open on rusty hinges. They played their flashlights around the room and spotted nothing amiss. Crawling out of their sleeping bags, they explored throughout the house and discovered the recently attached door standing ajar. Closing it again, one of the hunters secured it with the rusty latch hook. The next morning, both hunters were surprised to see the same door standing wide open.

Night after night for as long as the two men remained in the cabin, the door refused to stay closed. Spooked by the experience, they abandoned the structure and never returned.

Today, deep in the woods of Newton County, the logs of the Tolliver cabin, as it is still called, have weathered to a grayish hue typical of an aged wooden structure. Abandoned for many years now, the roof of the dwelling has partially collapsed, and some of the chinking has fallen from the spaces between the logs.

To the occasional hiker or deer hunter who passes this way and encounters the fallen down cabin, it appears quite uninhabited and looks as though no one has lived there for a long, long time. Old-timers in the area, however, are quick to point out that someone, or something, still resides in the house. And they tell anyone who suggests they might use it as a hunting cabin to make certain they don't close the door to the bedroom, for Old Man Tolliver's ghost lives there and it might want to get out.

The Haunted Room

Newton County, Arkansas, is the location of yet another strange tale of a door that wouldn't remain closed. This odd activity was accompanied by an occasional pounding that disturbed occupants of the house almost every night.

Sometime during the month of April in the early 1900s, an elderly couple moved into an old cabin set back in a remote hollow in the northern part of Newton County. The structure, expertly made of logs, contained three rooms and a stone fireplace, and was floored with hand-hewn planks fitted tightly together. The cabin had been abandoned for several years.

The previous occupants of the cabin were two men who earned a meager living as commercial hunters and trappers. One was named Martin and the other was known only as "Hook" because he wore a metal hook attached to his left arm where his hand, as he once explained, had been blown away in a mining accident. Though no one knows for certain, it is believed the man named Martin constructed the cabin.

From time to time, Martin and Hook would arrive at a nearby settlement to purchase supplies and, without spending much time in conversation with anyone, return to the deep woods. Two or three years later, only Martin would show up in town. When he was questioned by the locals about his partner, Martin was evasive, saying only that Hook was "back in the woods."

A rumor surfaced that Martin and Hook had some kind of disagreement and that the two men, once friends, became bitter enemies. Whatever the truth, Hook was never seen again, and Martin remained unresponsive to questions regarding his old friend's whereabouts.

One autumn, Martin was spotted leaving the region. He was last seen guiding two mules that were pulling a heavily laden wagon down a rutted trail that led toward the southwest. He told a passerby that he was going to Texas and that he didn't know if he would return or not.

Several weeks later when three area residents passed by Martin's cabin during a bear hunt, they noted that it was unoccupied. On investigation, they found it to be completely abandoned.

An elderly couple eventually moved into the long-deserted cabin, used one of the rooms for a bedroom, another for a kitchen and living area, and the third for storage.

After living in the cabin for about two months, the new residents began experiencing an odd and unexplainable series of events associated with one of the rooms. Initially, a strange, muffled pounding was heard coming from the storage room. The noise awakened the couple late one night, and the old man got up to investigate. After unlatching the eyehook that secured the wooden door to the room, he entered and stopped to listen, but the noise ceased.

About two hours after returning to bed, he heard the sound again. He finally decided the noise must have come from some kind of animal outside the cabin and he concerned himself about it no more. But each night the noise started again, and each time the old man re-entered the seldom-used storage room during the next few weeks in response to the strange pounding, the noise immediately ceased. The odd sound continued throughout the summer, but the man and woman grew accustomed to it and, after a time, were able to ignore it altogether.

One evening, however, the pounding was much louder than ever before, causing the residents to awaken with a start. Once again, the old man unlatched the door and entered the storage room. This time, however, the noise did not cease, and the man was unnerved to realize that the sound was coming from beneath the floor! The sound continued for nearly one-half hour before finally stopping. Later, he told a friend that the noise sounded like someone pounding at the lid of a casket as if trying to get out.

That was the last time the couple heard the pounding, but what followed was to cause them even greater concern. Late one evening as the two lay in bed, they heard the distinctive sound of the eyehook that secured the storeroom door flipping open. This was quickly followed by the creaking sound of a door opening on rusted hinges. Too frightened to get out of bed to investigate, the couple lay together huddled quietly and waiting to see what would happen next.

Nothing did, and presently the old man got up and went to examine the door. It was standing wide open! He closed it, secured the latch, and went back to bed. Fifteen minutes later, the eyehook snapped open once again and the door creaked open, this time banging loudly against the wall. The couple got no sleep that night.

The following morning, the old man closed and latched the storeroom door and nailed a stout board across it. That, he believed, would put an end once and for all to the strange occurrence. But it didn't.

That evening after the two had retired to bed and fallen asleep, they were suddenly awakened by the loud sound of the board falling to the floor. This was followed by the all-too-familiar sounds of the eyehook opening and the door slamming open.

Two weeks later, the man and woman packed up their belongings and moved out of the house. They purchased another dwelling not far from the community of Jasper near the Buffalo River. They never returned to the old cabin back in the hollow, but they told the story of the strange haunting to any and all who would listen to them.

About one year later, two teenage boys decided to hike into the hollow and visit what came to be known among Jasper residents as a haunted house. On arriving at the old cabin, they found it had burned down. As the boys poked through the debris and ashes, they kicked apart some pieces of what were appeared to be flooring. When they looked beneath the planks, they received the shock of their lives. Partially buried in the dirt beneath the planks was a skeleton!

The boys immediately alerted the sheriff's office, and within a few days, investigators arrived at the site of the old cabin. After removing charred floor and logs and sweeping away a layer of ash and forest debris, they uncovered a complete, yet highly deteriorated, skeleton. A remarkable feature of this skeleton was, attached to the left arm, a rusted metal hook.

The skeleton found beneath the floor of the old cabin was clearly that of the man called Hook. What is not known is how he came to be there. Most believe he was killed by Martin and hidden under the cabin floor, but too much time has passed for the truth to ever be revealed.

Perhaps a more pertinent question is: Was the ghost of the man buried beneath the wooden floor responsible for the strange sounds coming from the storeroom and the unlatching of the door? Many believe it was.

Taney County Haunting

Not far from the shores of Lake Taneycomo near the town of Branson, Missouri, can be found a house which continues to manifest a curious haunting to this day. This southwestern Missouri Ozarks community is rich in lore and legend, and many of the long-time residents who can recall the tale of this strange haunting claim it is one of the region's greatest unsolved mysteries.

During the 1930s, a curious stranger arrived in Branson. He checked into one of the hotels and undertook a quest to purchase a house. The stranger was dressed in expensive, tailored clothes, and was seldom seen without a black silk vest and carrying a gold pocket watch attached to a gold chain. He wore a fashionable black derby hat, and some of the Branson residents commented that he looked like a gambler.

Eventually, the stranger found a house to his liking and purchased it, paying the full amount in cash. The house was a two-story Victorian-style structure, well cared for, and located only a short walk from the White River, a portion of which has been damned to form today's Lake Taneycomo.

The stranger lived in the house for about two years, rarely venturing out into town and seldom conversing with the local residents. It appeared as though he disdained any kind of relationship with the locals, and often went out of his way to avoid them. According to neighbors, he never received guests. One day, the stranger was seen boarding an outbound train at the depot, leaving his house in the care of a deaf handyman who did odd jobs around town.

Two weeks later, the stranger returned, and when he stepped off the train he was accompanied by an attractive woman several years younger than he. She appeared quite reserved and no more inclined to speak with the residents of the town than he. Within a few days, it somehow became known that she was his wife and that they had recently married somewhere in Illinois.

The wife was occasionally seen around town shopping for groceries and sundries, and sometimes just out for a walk. She particularly liked to stroll along the bank of the stream. When she was approached by her neighbors, she was always friendly and pleasant, but remained somewhat distant and evasive. She never allowed herself to get close to anyone. Though often invited to teas and parties and other gatherings, the couple always declined.

Other than their self-inflicted reclusiveness, the couple attracted little or no attention. They always paid their bills on time and were never known to bother anyone. Because of their rather solitary way of life, it did not seem unusual that weeks would sometimes pass without Branson residents spotting their somewhat quiet and evasive neighbors.

Then, for several months in a row, only the man of the house was seen. In fact, it was noticed that the husband now did all of the shopping. When Branson residents got together to talk about such things, it occurred to them they had not seen the woman in over six months. They thought that was curious.

The townsfolk were not the only ones interested in the whereabouts of the young woman. Her parents in Illinois contacted the local police chief inquiring of her whereabouts—it turned out they had not heard from her for a long time and were growing concerned.

When the police chief visited the home of the reclusive couple to inquire, the husband answered the door and told him that his wife was fine, that she had recently left town to visit some relatives in Iowa.

Eventually, a full year passed without anyone seeing or hearing from the young woman. One day, her parents arrived in Branson by train, sought directions to the home of their daughter and her husband, and walked immediately to the address. After receiving no response to their knock, they went to the office of the local police chief and requested his help. Together, the parents, the police chief, and two policemen returned to the house.

After several more minutes of knocking on the front door, the police chief finally ordered his subordinates to break it open. On entering, it was clear that someone had apparently left in a hurry and had been gone for quite some time. Clothes were scattered around, unwashed dishes were still in the sink, and windows hadn't even been closed. Rain from previous storms had blown into the house, causing some small amount of damage to rugs and curtains. A thorough search of the house failed to yield any information on the former occupants or clues relative to what might have become of them.

The parents of the girl remained in Branson for several weeks, hoping for the return of their daughter, but as time passed they grew concerned that something terrible must have happened to her. On several occasions the police allowed them to enter the house and search for any evidence that might suggest what happened to the couple.

One afternoon, the daughter's mother was looking through some items in the cellar when she noticed a low mound of dirt. On closer inspection, it appeared that a portion of the cellar floor had been excavated and then replaced. It looked, in fact, much like a grave. Fearing the worst, she called her husband and, within the hour, the two had alerted the police chief to their discovery.

As the parents watched, two policemen dug into the mound of dirt. A few minutes later, a body was lifted out of a shallow grave. It was the body of the daughter.

A warrant was subsequently issued for the arrest of the husband. He was described in the document as being in his mid-fifties with dark eyes and a head of thick, grey hair. His manner of dress was also described, including the silk vest, the gold pocket watch, and the black derby hat. A man who bore a remarkable resemblance to the husband was spotted in New Orleans several weeks later, but when authorities arrived to question him, he disappeared. The warrant remained active for years, but the husband was never found.

Years passed, and the house occupied by the mysterious couple changed owners several times.

Sometime during the 1970s, the occupants of the house at that time were hosting a party. One of the guests asked to use the bathroom and was directed to one located on the second floor. Moments after she entered and closed the door, the guest was surprised and utterly frightened to discover someone, a man, was watching her through the window. Screaming, she fled from the bathroom, down the stairs, and excitedly reported the incident to the party-goers in the great room. Quickly, several people hurried up to the bathroom to see what they could find out.

It was soon discerned that anyone peeping into the second floor bathroom window would have been at least ten feet off the ground, and there were no handholds, footholds, or ladders for such a thing to be possible. A search of the house and the premises failed to turn up any sign of an intruder.

The woman who had been surprised by the peeper remained adamant that someone had looked into the bathroom window. So concerned were she and the owners of the house, that the police were summoned.

When asked to provide a description of the peeper, the young woman said he appeared to be in his fifties, possessed a shock of grey hair covered by a black derby, was wearing a black silk vest, and carrying a gold pocket watch.

During the following decades, the mysterious intruder appeared several more times—sometimes he was seen looking into second floor windows, others times he was spotted at ground level. On one occasion he was actually seen moving about inside the house, and on another he was observed walking around in the yard. In every case, he was identified as having grey hair and wearing a black silk vest with a gold chain dangling from the pocket.

Most Branson residents aware of this haunting are convinced the ghostly figure is that of the eccentric man who lived in the house during the 1930s. They are likewise convinced he killed his wife and buried her in the basement.

Why his ghost continues to haunt the house, however, no one has the slightest idea, and the mystery continues to baffle and intrigue residents and visitors alike.

Harding University's Mysterious Ghost

Though it is not heard as frequently as it was during the 1970s, some citizens in the White County town of Searcy, Arkansas, particularly those living near the Ozark foothills campus of Harding University, still talk about the ghost. This ghost has never been seen, only heard, and it is a ghost that plays the piano.

A few long-time employees of this small private school still relate tales of the spooky happenings. As they tell it, people passing by the music building late at night would occasionally hear the soft refrains of a piano being played, the sound coming from the third floor. On investigation, no one could be found—all the rooms on that floor were vacant and all the entrances were securely locked.

But there is more to the story, say the old-timers, and this is how they explain the mysterious piano-playing ghost of Harding University.

Many years ago, two students—a young man and a young woman who were sweethearts in high school—came to the college to pursue degrees in music. They spent practically every waking moment together, and when they were not attending classes, studying for exams, or practicing the piano, they could often be seen walking in the moonlight, surreptitiously holding hands. They had to be cautious about showing affection, for at the time, such things were frowned upon at that rather conservative church school. The two talked often about their plans—they intended earn their degrees, get married, have children, and secure jobs teaching music.

Several weeks into the first semester, the young man died in a horrible automobile wreck. The young woman, grief stricken, found it very difficult to concentrate on her studies and spent the days and nights in her dormitory room crying.

On those rare occasions when she left her room, the girl would walk to the old music building, climb the stairs to the third floor, let herself into one of the practice rooms, and play the piano. For hours at a time she engaged herself thus, and people passing by on the sidewalk below would sometimes pause to listen to her skilled performances.

As the semester progressed, the young woman, preoccupied with the tragic loss of the boy she loved, fell far behind in her studies and her grades consequently suffered. Friends were unable to cheer her up and counselors were unable to soothe her grief or help her focus attention on her classes. It appeared to them she had lost all reason for living.

One morning, they found her dead in her dormitory room. While a clinical explanation was provided for her passing, close acquaintances knew she simply wasted away from the sorrow of losing the boy she loved so much.

On the night the girl died, several people walking by the music building heard the sound of a piano being played. The music came from the third floor, even though all the lights were out. The playing, they claimed, was easily recognized by those who heard it as that of the young woman. On investigation, however, the floor was found to be empty, and the doors to the rooms were locked!

For years thereafter, students and faculty passing by the music building at night often reported hearing the sounds of a piano playing on the third floor. Each time the source of the music was investigated, no one was found. In most cases, all of the doors were locked securely. Eventually, they determined, it was the ghost of the young girl that was playing the piano.

Even today, some who are not familiar with this tale claim to hear piano music while passing a certain location on the campus.

The chilling part of this tale is related to the fact that the old three-story music building was torn down and replaced by a newer structure, this one only two stories tall!

Today, late in the evening when one stands near an open window on the second floor of the new building, one can sometimes hear the soft sounds of a piano, a haunting, gentle music.

And the sound comes from somewhere above.

The Widow's Rocking Chair

Here and there, deep in the Oklahoma Ozark Mountains in Delaware County, can be found isolated, small clusters of homes, most of them old, some new. Most of the older homes are located on farms and ranches, others are found on small acreages purchased by retirees and those who simply crave a rural lifestyle and want to live in a country environment.

Around the turn of the century and for some years thereafter, residents of this area earned their living mostly from farming and ranching. When they went into town, which wasn't often, they generally purchased items they were unable to raise on the farm, such as coffee, sugar, and other staples, as well as equipment such as harnesses and tools. While the economy in this region never boomed, it was quite adequate for those who chose to live there.

During the late 1960s, an elderly resident of this area, a long-time cattle rancher, lived in the same house that had once been occupied by his parents. The old house was a frame structure fashioned expertly from milled timber which was cut from the nearby hills. The house had been well-kept over the years—coats of paint were applied regularly and repairs and additions were made when necessary.

The rancher, a widower, grew too aged and infirm to get around much by himself. With encouragement from his grown children and grandchildren, he finally decided it was time to move into town and live with a family member. As a result of his decision, he put the house and farm up for sale. Along with the house, the old man decided to sell some his furniture, including an old rocking chair which he said was his wife's favorite. The old rancher explained to prospective buyers how his late wife would sit in the chair facing the bedroom window, and rock for hours as she knitted, quilted, or soothed a sick child.

While closing the deal with the eventual buyer, the old man, just before being driven away by a nephew, explained to the new owners that the house was haunted by the ghost of his dead wife. She was a pleasant ghost, he said, never malicious or frightening. When she passed away, he told the buyers, she was considerably younger than he, and her ghost always appeared as a young, beautiful woman wearing a long, flowing, white gown.

When the new owner moved in with his wife and two young sons a week later, he rearranged much of the furniture left by the old man. He left the rocking chair in the bedroom, however, stating that it seemed like it belonged there.

Several months later, the new owner's two sons, along with a friend, were playing the back yard. Growing hungry and thirsty, the three boys entered the kitchen through the back door in search of a snack and something cool to drink. As they passed the hallway which led to the master bedroom, the friend saw a young woman dressed in a long white gown walking toward him. A moment later when he joined his companions in the kitchen, he asked who she was. The brothers insisted no one else was in the house.

Later that same day, the two boys related the incident to their father, and he told them the story of the ghost that supposedly occupied the house. The father also instructed them not to believe in such things, they were simply the product of an overactive imagination.

During the next few years, the ghost of the pretty woman was seen several times by the brothers as well as by occasional guests, but, oddly, never by the parents. The father continued to insist there was no such thing as a ghost and refused to believe the house was haunted. He could not explain, however, why visitors to the house for the first time, visitors who were completely unaware of the haunting, sometimes mentioned seeing a young woman in a long gown walking down the hallway.

One afternoon, the father returned home from work early. Hearing what he thought was his wife in another part of the house, he called out, saying that he was going to prepare something to eat in the kitchen before going out to tend to some chores on the farm.

After making a sandwich, the father walked out the front door only to see his wife coming up the sidewalk! When he asked her who was in the house, she replied no one.

Cautiously, and considering it might be a burglar, the two re-entered the house. They went from room to room, checking each one thoroughly. When they arrived at the final room, the bedroom, they peered in. The first thing they saw, in the corner of the room facing the window, was the old chair. What surprised them and caused their flesh to prickle, however, was that it was rocking back and forth, but there was no one in it.

Thereafter, for the next ten years the family lived in the house, the rocker was seen moving under its own power many times. The father became a believer in ghosts, and eventually began to accept the woman in white one as a regular member of the family.

The Haunted Cabin

During the 1830's when most of the state of Missouri, and in particular the Ozark Mountains, was sparsely settled, Dr. Franklin Parker left his St. Louis home and a relatively important social position and traveled to the southwestern corner of the Show Me State where he intended to set up a new practice. Parker had grown weary of the big, bustling city, the boring lodge meetings, and the tedious dinner parties he was forced to attend. He craved the peace and quiet of a small settlement. A man who preferred the simple pleasures of life, Parker longed to conduct farming on a small scale, and perhaps begin a garden. He also wanted to reduce his patient load and spend more time with his wife and young daughter.

In southwestern Missouri not far from the present-day small town of Pineville, Parker found exactly what he and his wife were looking for—a pleasant environment, plenty of land for homesteading, fertile soil and an abundance of fresh water, and opportunities to start a farm. The few residents he encountered in the area seemed friendly enough and appeared to be sufficient to enable him to earn a decent living delivering babies and treating various infections and broken bones.

Everything the Parker family owned was packed into a sturdy wagon. In the front seat, Parker negotiated the two harnessed mules along the rough and bumpy roads that led into the rugged and rocky Ozarks, the wagon creaking along behind. On one side of Parker in the front seat was his wife, Anna, and on the other, his young daughter, Mary. Following a long and tiring journey, the Parkers finally arrived at their destination—a small settlement located along the banks of the Elk River. They were happy and relieved the trip was finally over and were eager to begin their new life in this new setting.

It rained constantly during the final two days of the long journey, and little Mary, only six-years-old, had taken quite ill and was running a high fever that deeply concerned Parker. On arriving in Pineville, the physician pulled the wagon up to a small general store, climbed down, and went inside to inquire about temporary lodging. The owner of the store, J.T. Clement, visited with the Parkers for a few moments, welcomed them to the community, and eventually directed them to a double-pen log cabin about a half-mile down the road. Parker thanked Clement, climbed back into the wagon, and headed in the direction pointed out by the storekeeper. The doctor was anxious to get his daughter inside the cabin and out of the rain where he could care for her fever.

As he was carrying a heavy trunk from the wagon into one of the rooms of the cabin, Parker spotted a large, dark, dried bloodstain on the wooden plank floor. Not wanting his wife and child to be alarmed by the spot, he placed the trunk on top of it so they would not see it. In the same room, Parker laid out a pallet for Mary and, right next to it, one for himself and his wife.

That night, Parker and his wife took turns caring for the sick girl, applying cold rags to her fevered brow and keeping her calm. Around midnight, as Parker cradled the youngster in his arm, she began thrashing about in a wild delirium.

At one point, the girl, clearly terrified, raised up, opened her eyes, and pointed a trembling finger toward the opposite side of the room where Parker had placed the trunk. In a quavering voice, the child described what she saw: Four men were playing cards at a table and they appeared to be angry with one another, for they were shouting and cursing. One of the men, according to the little girl, was a large bearded fellow wearing wide suspenders who suddenly pulled a knife from a leather scabbard and plunged it deep into the chest of another man. The victim fell to the floor, bleeding heavily, cried the girl.

When the child had finished her story, she collapsed in the arms of her father from the effort expended and slept relatively peacefully for the rest of the night.

The following morning, Parker drove the wagon back to Clement's store and purchased some sorely needed supplies. While he was paying for his goods, Parker told the merchant about his daughter's dream. Clement, who did not appear surprised at the tale, helped Parker carry his purchases outside to the wagon. When they had finished loading, the storekeeper told Parker an unusual story.

Several months earlier, said Clement, four strangers arrived in Pineville. They appeared to be trappers or prospectors and were looking for a place to stay for a few weeks before traveling on toward the west. One of the strangers was a big man with a heavy beard who wore wide suspenders and carried a large knife. The four men were directed to the same cabin in which Parker and his family were presently residing. The strangers seldom came to the store during the time they lived in the cabin, and passersby stated they often observed them through a window at night playing cards by lantern light.

One morning approximately three weeks following the arrival of the strangers, a passing resident noticed that the cabin appeared empty and he stopped to investigate. When he received no response to his knock on the door, he let himself in. He was immediately startled to find the body of one of the strangers stretched out on his back on the floor, a large knife sticking out of his chest. The dead man was never identified, and the other three strangers were never seen again.

Parker's flesh prickled at the story, for it so closely resembled portions of what his daughter described to him during her delirium of the previous night.

That evening, as Parker cradled Mary in his arms once again, her strange dream was repeated, almost identical to the one she had earlier. For the next two nights until she recovered from her fever, the youngster experienced the same troubling dream.

A few weeks later, the Parker family moved out of the log cabin and into a new home they had constructed not far away. Following the move, Mary's nightmares ceased. For as long as the Parkers lived in the area, they never ventured past the old double-pen log cabin in which they endured the haunting experience.

For years, residents living near the old log cabin commented on hearing strange noises emanating from the structure late at night, noises that sounded like men arguing and fighting. Sometimes passersby mentioned seeing a lantern light inside the cabin and observing four men playing cards at a rickety wooden table, but as the passersby came closer to the cabin the images would disappear, gradually fading from sight similar to mist blown away by the wind.

The double-pen log cabin burnt down many decades ago. To this day, however, some long-time southwestern Missouri residents claim the site where the structure once stood is still haunted. Late at night, they say, four men dressed in early nineteenth century garb are sometimes seen seated around a wooden table playing cards, the entire image floating just above the ground where the old cabin once stood.

And when one approaches the image, it swirls away in the night air, disappearing among the nearby trees.

Oklahoma Ozarks Haunted House

Not far from the small town of Jay in northeastern Oklahoma's Delaware County, there is a large farmhouse that has served as the setting for a series of strange hauntings by several different ghosts for many years. Though research and investigation have been conducted on several different occasions, to this day no one has ever learned anything substantive about the history of the ghosts or why the structure remains haunted.

A long time ago, the old farmhouse was owned by an elderly lady named Woodcock. Mrs. Woodcock, twice-widowed, was a woman of means and could have lived anywhere she pleased, but she chose to stay in the haunted place. She had grown up in this area and still had relatives living nearby.

Many times, Mrs. Woodcock once told a friend, she climbed the stairs to retire to her second floor bedroom only to encounter three or four ghostly forms at the top of the landing. The spirits always seemed to be involved in animated conversation, perhaps arguing with one another, but she could never quite hear any of the words distinctly. The ghosts were all males and were dressed in the garb of Civil War-era soldiers, according to Mrs. Woodcock, but she could not determine whether they belonged to the Union or the Confederacy. She was under the impression they were all officers, but she could never explain why she thought so. The ghosts, which appeared almost nightly, were completely oblivious to her presence until she came to within six feet of them, at which point they would simply vanish into the adjacent walls, scattering quickly like quail flushed in a meadow.

Mrs. Woodcock was never threatened or harmed by the ghosts in her house, and over time she gradually grew accustomed to their visits.

In addition to Mrs. Woodcock's bedroom, there was another one on the second floor which was never used. An oft-told story, learned by Mrs. Woodcock when she moved into the house several years earlier, told of the murder of a young woman in that room sometime during the Civil War.

The woman, according to one version of the tale, was betrothed to a soldier, but while he was away during the war, she carried on an affair with a local man. One evening the soldier returned home unannounced and caught his fiancé in the arms of her lover and killed them both. The soldier was quickly sent away to some location in Tennessee by his superiors, but it was rumored that the woman's two brothers tracked him down and killed him. The actual identities of the woman, her lover, and the soldier have been lost with the passage of so much time.

The door to that particular bedroom, for reasons never explained, would never stay closed. Though Mrs.

Woodcock would personally see to it that it was shut each night, the door would always be open the following morning. Sometimes the door would mysteriously pop open within seconds after Woodcock closed it. Mrs. Woodcock once employed a handyman to fix the door so it would remain shut, but despite his efforts, the door would be found open in the morning.

Though Mrs. Woodcock never saw it, guests in her house sometimes reported seeing the ghost of a young woman walking down the second floor hallway and entering a bedroom. When the guests peered into the bedroom, no one was there.

Approximately halfway down the long hallway was a full-length mirror. The mirror, an antique about five-and-a-half-feet tall was expertly bound in a handsomely carved and sculpted wooden frame and mounted on a swivel such that it could be positioned by the different guests who used it. The mirror, like the rest of the second floor, was haunted.

Occasionally, the glass surface of this mirror would be covered with an opaque, pasty substance that was very difficult to remove. The pasty film never appeared on any other surface in the house—only on that particular mirror. Only repeated washings with a strong solvent would rid the mirror of the film. Though many people have seen the substance that formed upon and clung to the surface of the mirror, no one was ever able to identify it or explain its appearance. The story is told that some of the substance was sent to a university in New Jersey for analysis, but no response was ever received.

Another odd phenomenon associated with the old farmhouse was the unexplained aroma of roses. Throughout the year, but particularly during the month of February, the house was rich with the strong scent of roses, even though there were no flowers in the house at all. The aroma permeated every room and guests often commented on it. Like the strange substance on the mirror, there was no explanation whatsoever for the scent of roses.

Every once in a while, Mrs. Woodcock claimed that pictures hanging from the walls of the house would be tilted at a variety of angles. Sometimes, she said, when she entered the great room in the morning the pictures on the walls were completely rearranged. Woodcock would spend several minutes replacing the pictures on their assigned hooks only to find them changed around the next morning.

Though initially bothered by the ghosts and hauntings in her home, Mrs. Woodcock gradually grew accustomed to them, even referring to them as her "playful pranksters" that lived with her.

Mrs. Woodcock passed away many years ago, and her home is currently occupied by one of her nephews and his family. The house, they claim, is still haunted in the exact same manner as described by Mrs. Woodcock. But like Mrs. Woodcock, they have come to accept the spirits as residents of the old home and have managed to live in peace with them.

The mirror was moved out of the house and given to another relative. Since that time, the mysterious opaque film has never appeared on the glass.

Satan's House

A few miles east of the town of West Plains in the gently rolling Ozark hills of Missouri can be found the remains of a house that was once considered by many as a residence of Satan. Some claim that, even after the passage of several decades, the devil continues to roam the grounds of the former of location of the strange house.

Many years ago in Oregon County, Missouri, a young man inherited a sizeable sum of money from a recently deceased uncle. With the money, the nephew, who resided in an old log cabin with his wife and two children, decided to have a new house constructed, a fine home for him and his family. At the first opportunity, he began making the necessary arrangements by purchasing materials and hiring carpenters.

Within days, workmen were busy constructing the new house about fifty yards from the log residence. Since the location was several miles from the nearest town, the carpenters were allowed to live on the premises during the week, each of them returning to their homes and families on the weekends.

About two weeks before the new house was to be completed, one of the carpenters quit, telling the nephew that the place was haunted. He explained further that during the night strange noises awakened the workers. The sounds included a rhythmic hammering on the walls accompanied by the opening and closing of doors that had been tightly latched. The worker suggested to the nephew that the house was cursed and warned him not to move into it. The house, he said, was occupied by Satan.

The nephew dismissed the carpenter's claim as foolish, paid him off, and sent him on his way. Two days later, however, the rest of the carpenters quit, claiming the house was haunted and they would stay near it a moment longer. It was the devil, they insisted.

The nephew simply hired other carpenters, and in time the structure was completed. One of the newer workers also complained to the nephew about the strange noises and sightings in the house and suggested that it was haunted. Still, the nephew refused to believe such a thing was possible.

The nephew recalled warnings, however, on the first night after he and his family moved into the new house. Describing the experience many years later, he stated that the home creaked and moaned during the entire night. Initially, he attributed the odd noises to the fact that the timbers in the recently constructed house were settling, but when doors began opening and slamming shut on their own, he knew something more was occurring, something bizarre and frightening. The doors, he discovered later, had been latched and locked, but somehow still managed to open.

The next morning, the nephew's wife stepped into the kitchen only to discover that objects earlier placed in the cabinets and on shelves had spilled out onto the floor. Several dishes and glasses were broken and flatware was strewn across the table.

Night after night it was the same and the family got very little sleep. After two weeks of being subjected to the ongoing haunting of the new house, the nephew and his family moved back into the modest log cabin.

About two weeks later as the nephew pondered about what to do with this new house in which he was unable to live, he was paid a visit by the first carpenter who had resigned and provided the warning that the house was occupied by Satan. The carpenter told the nephew that he was in constant contact with the devil, and that for a sum of money he could rid the house of evil spirits. The nephew refused this offer and sent the man away once again. The hauntings continued unabated for the next several years.

One evening while the nephew and his family were away on a trip to St. Louis, the house burned to the ground. When they returned, the family could still see a thin, wispy plume of smoke rising from the ashes. All that was left of the house were the foundation, the stout rock chimney, and a few boards and doors that escaped the inferno.

Several months later, the nephew decided to have yet another house constructed on a plot of ground several yards from the previous one. As much as possible, he salvaged some materials from the recently destroyed house, including rocks from the foundation and chimney as well as one of the doors.

Though the recycled door could be latched and secured with a sliding bolt, it would fly open at night, apparently of its own accord, and then, just as suddenly, slam shut with a great noise and with such force that it shook the entire structure. Nothing the nephew did could keep the door from opening and closing on its own.

Finally, after putting up with the leftover haunting of the slamming door, the nephew removed it from the hinges, took it outside, and burned it. In its place, he installed a brand new door. From that point on, the nephew and his family were never disturbed again, at least, not in the new house.

Around the remains of the old house, however, strange sightings occurred. The nephew and his wife sometimes spotted odd figures and shapes roaming about the former home site and the surrounding grounds well into the night. The first time he saw them, the nephew lit a lantern, grabbed his rifle, and went to investigate. He came up behind what he initially believed was a trespasser and shouted at it. The figure turned and glared at the nephew with, as he said later, "glowing red eyes." Terrified, the nephew dropped his rifle and the lantern and fled screaming back to the new house.

When he regained his composure, he told his wife that he had just stared into the face of Satan!

Ghost House of the Ozarks

Sometime during the early 1980s, a writer spent several weeks traveling many of the remote back roads of the Ozark Mountains in search of interviews with old-time residents. He was in the business of collecting and writing about folk tales, folk music, and folk medicines, and he discovered that the Ozark denizens represented a wealth of untapped information pertinent to such lore. Besides, as he stated later, the environment was pleasant and the scenery was beautiful.

On this particular trip, which took him along the dirt back roads of Searcy County in Northern Arkansas, the writer steered his pick-up truck down what was an apparently seldom used, rutted path in a little traveled section of the thickly wooded mountains.

After a time, it occurred to him that he was lost, and he eventually gave up trying to locate the residence of a potential interview and devoted himself to trying to find his way back to a paved road and civilization.

At a fork in the dirt road, the writer selected the left branch. After driving slowly along this section of the road, he began to realize he had made a mistake—the ruts were eroded deeper here and the profusion of weeds, shrubs, and small saplings growing between them was a clear indication few people ever passed this way. The brush was scraping and slapping against the underside of his vehicle. He persevered, however, and soon found himself in a beautiful yet extremely isolated section of the forest that looked as if it had not been visited by human beings for two hundred years. The thick tangle of underbrush between the closely spaced trees was so dense as to be impenetrable, and a thick canopy of leafy branches grew over the road such that the sunlight barely made its way through. It seemed almost as if he were driving through a cave. The dim, diffused light that managed to filter through the forest canopy dappled the leaf-littered forest floor, providing for an eerie, shadowy texture, leaving the impression of being underwater. Unused to such a spectacle, the writer grew nervous and sought a way to turn his vehicle around and return in the direction from which he had come.

As he proceeded down the trail in search of a wide place to negotiate a turn, he spotted an old, abandoned two-story structure located about fifty feet off the road. A dense growth of vines climbed the sides of the house, all struggling to meet at the apex of the peaked roof.

The writer stopped his truck, turned off the engine, and exited for a closer look. As he stood beside his pick-up, wiping the perspiration from his face, he was unprepared for the sudden silence that greeted him, a silence unbroken by the chirp of a bird or the buzz of an insect, a silence that was deep and dark, and just a little scary.

Pushing through tall grass and weeds—all the while hoping he would not encounter a snake—the writer made his way toward the old house. His footsteps sounded uncommonly loud against the stark silence of the woods. Here and there, just out of the range of his vision, small, unidentified creatures scurried through the dense grass, each sudden movement and sound causing him to jump and make his heart race faster. Though a bit frightened, he continued toward the old structure.

The wooden porch creaked loudly when he stepped on it, but it appeared solid. Approaching the front door, he knocked timidly and then realized how foolish it was to even consider such a thing. Clearly, the place had been abandoned for decades. The front door likewise responded noisily when he pushed it open to look inside.

Enough light filtered through the broken windows and the open door to slightly illuminate the lower floor, which consisted of a living room and kitchen.

More unseen creatures scurried about in the semi-darkness, disappearing around corners or cracks in the walls. He stepped onto the debris-covered floor.

The walls were papered with old newspapers, apparently several layers deep, and he recalled that was how early settlers here attempted to insulate their house against the cold. He scanned the newspapers and the most recent issue he could find was dated 1931.

The entire room was bare and completely devoid of any furniture except, oddly, for an upright piano that was set against the far wall. Kicking through the accumulation of rotted leaves and brittle branches that littered the floor to a depth of a couple of inches, he walked over to the instrument.

Strangely, the piano had only a light covering of dust on its surface. He struck one of the keys and jumped back in surprise when a clear, crisp note rang throughout the room. He struck another key, then another. Then he made chords. Remarkably, he thought, all of the keys functioned. Even more remarkably, the piano was in tune!

The writer pondered the few piano tunes he knew. He dusted off the old wooden stool, sat before the keys, and began a slow-tempo rendition of "Precious Memories." The sound filled the house, reverberating off the walls and diffusing into the forest. When he completed the tune, the writer paused to listen to the fading strains of the final notes. Then he undertook to play "Amazing Grace" and performed a fair rendition, actually singing along during the last verse and chorus.

He lost track of the time as he sat before the old piano and played one tune after another. Finally, perceiving that it was growing darker, he rose from the stool and stepped outside. He looked toward the west and discerned that the sun was setting on what little horizon that was visible through the maze of woods. The already dark forest was growing murky and he decided he'd best leave now while there was still a little bit of daylight left.

It took the writer approximately thirty minutes to travel about five miles of very difficult trail, but he finally came out onto a stretch of graded road he remembered from earlier in the day. Just a little over a half-mile down this road, he came to another house, this one with a lighted interior and a new pick-up truck parked outside.

He stopped, got out of his vehicle, walked to the front door, and knocked. Presently, the door opened and a man in his fifties stood before him, his face reflecting curiosity at who might be calling at this late hour.

The resident, judging from his tractor cap and overalls, was a farmer. The writer introduced himself, explained that he was lost, and asked for directions to the nearby town of St. Joe where he intended to spend the night. After the farmer provided the information, the writer, pointing back from where he had just come, asked him about the old house in the woods.

The farmer narrowed his eyes a bit as he stared at the visitor, tilted his head ever so slightly, and said he wasn't aware of any other house in the area. The writer described the vine-covered wood-frame structure and told him about the piano in the living room. The farmer continued to look at him intently, took a deep breath, then stepped out onto the porch to stand next to him. As he spoke, his gaze was fixed on the woods that started just beyond his field.

"I've lived in this place for over forty years," he said. "I've farmed this land and hunted these woods nearly all my life. I probably know every inch of this area for miles around." The farmer paused, looked directly at the writer, and said, "I'm tellin' you, there ain't no house out in them woods."

He continued in a deeper tone, now looking at the ground as he spoke, as if unsure of himself. "You ain't the first person to stop by here and mention that house. There have been others." He looked up and spoke with confidence, "But, that house just doesn't exist."

The writer didn't know what to say. He thought at first he wanted to try to convince the farmer about the existence of the house, but he was afraid of angering him. During a long pause, it occurred to him the farmer was speaking the truth, or at least he was convinced he was speaking the truth.

The silence became uncomfortable, Presently, the farmer spoke again. "I have to tell you this. Some nights when it's real still and there ain't no wind or nothin', from far off in that direction where you just come from, you can hear piano music comin' through the trees, kinda soft-soundin' music, kinda strange and waverin', comin' and goin', and then it eventually stops."

Looking out into the woods, the farmer said, "but we ain't ever been able to figure out where it's comin' from."

After a bit more conversation, the writer thanked the farmer for his time and the directions, climbed into his truck, and drove away. For the next few hours, he was troubled by the notion that he had just experienced a ghost house.

On two occasions during the next year, the writer returned to the same area in an attempt to relocate the house, to visit it, and to play the piano once again. He wanted to prove to himself that he really saw what he thought he saw and try to experience once again what happened previously. He left the paved road at the exact same point and he drove along what he was convinced were the same dirt back roads. He was even convinced he encountered the identical deeply rutted trail with weeds and low-growing bushes growing between the tracks.

But he could not find the house!

Almost twenty years have passed since the writer's original experience with what he calls the Ghost House of the Ozarks. The experience, he maintains, was real.

The house? The writer is now convinced that the house itself is a ghost, and like most spirits it is seen when it wants to be seen and remains invisible when it is necessary to do so.

The piano presents yet another mystery. Why, wonders the writer, was the piano in the old house. Did it belong to the former occupants? Why did they not take it with them when they moved away? Furthermore, why was the piano relatively free from dust and an accumulation of other debris when everything else in the house was covered with it? Was someone using the piano regularly? And was that someone another ghost?

the
Haunted Countrysides

Old Raw Head and Bloody Bones

An oft-told tale throughout much of the southeastern Missouri Ozark Mountains is that of Old Raw Head. During the past hundred years or so that this story has been related, it has evolved into a variety of forms, has been assigned different endings and characters, and is placed in several different locations in the Ozark Mountains of Missouri. Nevertheless, year in and year out the narrative essentially maintains some level of consistency, and is still frequently heard today. Some say it is only a tale, others maintain that it actually happened.

Many decades ago in some deep, dark hollow in the Missouri Ozarks, an old woman lived alone save for a single constant companion—a large wild razorback hog.

The woman was regarded as a witch by the few that encountered her, and she was sometimes seen cooking up concoctions of roots, herbs, bat's wings, and a number of unidentifiable things in a huge black iron cauldron. Believing she had the ability to cure certain maladies, some of the mountain residents would occasionally venture into the hollow and cautiously approach the old woman and request medicines. She would listen to descriptions of their ailments and, wordlessly, provide each of the visitors with some kind of remedy and send them on their way. The old woman never charged anyone for her potions, but a few who could afford to do so would leave a coin now and then.

Those who came and sought her remedies remained quite afraid of her. Though no one ever actually saw it happen, tales circulated through the region that the old woman could make someone disappear merely by muttering an incantation.

If they were afraid of the old woman, they were even more afraid of her pig—a huge, vicious-looking razorback hog that snuffled and grunted angrily at any and all visitors. The hog followed the old woman everywhere she went, even into the tiny house.

It was clear the old woman cared deeply for the hog. She always saw to its comfort and made certain it always had plenty to eat. The relationship between the old woman and the hog was indeed strange.

One afternoon, two young brothers out squirrel hunting were hiking through this rugged portion of the Ozarks when they entered the dark, narrow hollow occupied by the witch. Having heard wild stories about her and her hog but having never seen either, they crept toward the house, hiding in the thick stands of hickory and oak trees that proliferated throughout the bottom of the small canyon.

When the brothers, twelve and ten years of age respectively, got within thirty yards of the old woman's house, they spotted her stirring something in her cauldron which was set over a low fire. As they watched, hidden behind some low-growing brush, the old woman called to the hog and beckoned him to come over to the pot. When he arrived, she fed him some of the concoction she spooned out from within. To the utter surprise of the brothers, the hog, after slurping some of the contents of the pot, rose up on its two hind legs and walked and talked like a man.

Frightened beyond description, the two youngsters fled from their hiding place and related what they had seen to their parents. After this, hardly anyone ever ventured into the old woman's hollow again.

One autumn as the weather was turning cool, a man, riding an unsaddled swayback mule and carrying an old, rusted, and oft-repaired rifle, entered the hollow. He wore a red-checked shirt, denim overalls, and a floppy black felt hat. From the wear and tear evident in his clothes, it was clear the he was not a man of means, but rather one who was used to scraping out a living any way he could.

The man riding the mule was a newcomer to the region and had staked out a homestead three miles away in a neighboring hollow. The stranger had a wife and three children to feed. The thin and poor Ozark soils made it difficult to grow crops and the homesteader had no livestock save for a few chickens. He decided to forage through the woods in search of a wild hog he could kill and butcher to provide meat for the coming winter.

The stranger, being new to the region, had never heard of the old witch woman or her razorback hog. Presently, he spotted a large hog foraging among the acorn mast in a stand of oak trees by the narrow creek that ran through the hollow. Quietly, the man slid from the mule, crept through the trees until he found a suitable spot from which to shoot, and killed the hog.

Moments later, he had strung the carcass of the dead hog up to dangle from a stout limb and he proceeded to gut, skin, and butcher it. After removing most of the meat, he cut down the bloody skeleton of the hog. From the head, he cut away even more meat, meat that was to be used to make head cheese and scrapple. When he was finished, he cast the raw and bloody skull atop the pile of bones. By the time he tied the meat into the skin and fastened it securely onto the mule, the sun was beginning to set. Climbing atop the mule just behind the heavy load, the stranger guided the animal to the trail and rode out of the darkening hollow toward his home.

At precisely midnight, the raw, bloody hog skull suddenly jerked to and fro, paused, and then rolled off of the pile of bones. Instead of stopping, the skull continued to roll until it came to the tracks of the mule. There it stopped, right side up, and swiveled around, the empty eye-sockets directed back toward the pile of bones. All at once the head screamed, "Rise up, rise up, o' bloody bones!"

At this command, the pile of disjointed and bloody hog bones began trembling and vibrating. All of a sudden the pile fell apart and the individual bones appeared to be scrambling around in the dirt. Presently, each of the bones found the one it had been joined to in life, and ere long the entire skeleton of the razorback hog was completely reassembled. The skeleton then raced to the road where it was joined by the raw head. As a cloud drifted across the face of the moon, the raw head and bloody bones followed the track of the mule out of the hollow.

About two hours later, the head and bones arrived at the poor shack of the homesteader. The stranger, his wife, and three children were all asleep inside.

After a while, the man was awakened by strange noises outside his cabin. Rising from the bed, he peered out the window and could scarce believe his eyes as he gazed upon the raw head and bloody bones of a large razorback hog. On seeing the homesteader who killed and butchered him, the head emitted an unearthly scream, frightening the man and waking his family.

"Its' Raw Head and Bloody Bones," he screamed, "and he's come to get us."

As the family cowered in fear, huddled in a corner of the cabin, they heard the sound of Raw Head and Bloody Bones running around the house over and over. Eventually, the sound stopped, and all was quiet for several minutes.

Suddenly, the sounds started up again, but this time they were coming from the top of the house! The unmistakable sound of heavy footsteps on the roof terrified the family even more—old Raw Head and Bloody Bnes was stomping around on the cedar shingles just a few feet above their heads. This went on for several more minutes before finally stopping. Just when the homesteader thought the apparition had decided to leave, he heard a sound coming from inside his chimney. Sticking his head into the fireplace and peering up into the rock and clay void, the homesteader saw two yellow eyes staring back at him. The eyes looked like they were on fire.

Just as the homesteader pulled back out of the fireplace and rose to a standing position, old Raw Head and Bloody Bones scurried down the chimney and stood directly in front of him. Rearing up on its hind legs, the skeleton walked toward the frightened man, the angry eyes still burning yellow.

As quick as the strike of a rattlesnake, old Raw Head grabbed the homesteader in his powerful jaws, lifted him from the floor, and, carrying him as if he weighed no more than a small child, raced outside, tearing the door from its hinges as it went.

As the wife and children listened in horror, they heard the screams of the man fading away in the distance. They never saw him again.

In the morning when they dared to go outside, the wife discovered the mule had been killed—all that was left of it was a pile of bones, on top of which rested the hog's raw and bloody skull. Packing only what they could carry, the woman and the three children ran from the hollow on foot and fled from the area, never to return.

It is said that from time to time on still, moonlit nights, the occasional night traveler will see an unusual sight. It is sometimes reported that a skeleton of a razorback hog is seen trotting down the path that goes into a certain hollow. The skeleton is wearing a red-checked shirt, a pair of denim overalls, and a floppy black felt hat rest atop the raw head.

The Ghost of Crooked Creek

Crooked Creek, a stream long popular with canoeists and smallmouth bass fishermen, is located in the southern part of Boone County in northwestern Arkansas. The woodlands adjacent to the stream have also been a popular destination for fox, coon, squirrel, and deer hunters. In 1912, near the banks of Crooked Creek not far from the Newton County line, a young woman named Ella Barham was brutally murdered by a jealous suitor.

Every now and then, Ella Barham's ghost appears, a reminder of the horrible deed that was committed on that long ago afternoon.

About two years following the killing of Barham, a group of hunters reported seeing what they described as the ghost of a woman. The strange apparition appeared near a location known locally as Killebrew Ford. The ghost suddenly materialized before the men, its form gradually taking shape from the accumulating strands of mist hovering along the creek bank. The ghost stared at the hunters for several minutes, and then turned away. At that point, the shape disintegrated once again into fibers and strings of mist which slowly disappeared on the wind.

The ghost has been seen hundreds of times since then, and some local residents have claimed they even heard it speak.

In November, 1912, Ella Barham was on her way to visit a friend who lived near the confluence of Crooked Creek and West Fork. As was her habit, Ella rode her spirited mare, Brownie, along the trail that paralleled the stream.

Near Killebrew Ford, Ella encountered Odus Davidson who was cutting firewood. Odus was a local resident who had tried farming and failed and had difficulty holding down a job. At the time, he was earning a modest living cutting firewood for some elderly residents in the area. Odus had attempted to court Ella on several occasions, but was politely rejected each time. When Ella began seeing a man named Jim Greeson, Davidson grew furious and told friends he was going to kill her.

When Ella saw Davidson near the ford, she rode up to him and offered a greeting. Davidson, visibly angry and carrying his axe, approached Ella's horse and grabbed the bridle. As Ella tried to rein the animal away from Davidson, he dropped the axe and reached for her, grabbing her by the jacket and pulling her from the saddle. Once Ella was off the horse, Davidson threw her roughly to the ground. While Ella was attempting to stand, Davidson picked up his axe and brought it down solidly upon her head, splitting the skull open. Enraged, he continued to strike at the lifeless body until he eventually hacked it to pieces.

Not far away was an abandoned mine shaft, and, one by one, Davidson carried the pieces of the mutilated body into the tunnel to hide them.

Around noon, Ella's horse returned home, and relatives, concerned she may have had an accident, began to search for her.

That evening, a party of raccoon hunters were making their way along the Crooked Creek trail near Killebrew Ford when they heard the sounds of wild hogs rooting a short distance from the stream. Following the noise, they encountered several razorbacks trying to push their way into a pile of rocks just inside the old mine shaft. After two of the animals were shot and killed, the remainder of the pack fled, and the hunters approached the rock pile to see what the hogs were so interested in.

To their horror, the hunters found the mutilated limbs, torso, and head of Ella Barham. Before another two hours passed, law enforcement officers had been notified of the killing.

The next morning, the sheriff, accompanied by two deputies, went to the scene of the crime. Following a brief search of the area, one of the deputies found Davidson's axe which was partially hidden in some brush.

On the afternoon of the same day, the sheriff and his deputies rode up to the suspect's cabin. In his hands, the lawman carried a warrant for the arrest of Odus Davidson for the murder of Ella Barham.

When officers knocked on the front door, Davidson, who had watched the men approach the cabin, climbed out a rear window and fled in his stocking feet into the woods. The lawmen pursued him for a while, but Davidson, who knew the woods better than the lawmen, outdistanced them. The sheriff and his deputies, unable to keep up with Davidson, eventually gave up. The following morning, with the help of tracking dogs and volunteer searchers, Davidson was finally captured and placed in the county jail.

Following a brief trial, a jury found Odus Davidson guilty of murder and the judge ordered him hanged. Davidson, according to the available historical record, was the last man to be legally hanged in Arkansas.

For generations, the eerie ghost of Ella Barham has appeared before hundreds of eyewitnesses near Crooked Creek's Killebrew Ford, not far from where she was killed. Sightings have increased in recent years, as the creek has become a popular destination for bass fishermen and canoeists.

This image of the ghost of Ella Barham has been described by many over the years. Though the sightings have taken place over several decades and the ghost has been seen by dozens of people at different times, the descriptions remain consistent. Each time it appears, the ghost, though somewhat misty and opaque, is clearly that of a woman. When some of those who claimed to have seen the ghost were shown a photograph of Ella Barham, they all agreed it was the same woman.

The ghost of Ella Barham remains visible for only a few minutes before vanishing, and sometimes stunned watchers claim they can hear it calling out for help before it fades into the mist.

The Ghost of Petit Jean

Every once in a while, a curious ghost is seen atop Petit Jean Mountain, a pleasant low, wooded ridge located in central Arkansas' Conway County. The ghost that is seen here is believed to be that of a young woman, one who died on the mountain well over two hundred years ago. The ghost, though it occasionally frightens people, appears for only a short time, generally during the early evening, and then quickly vanishes. This strange apparition is a reminder of an amazing romance story, a special relationship between two lovers that came to a tragic and very sad ending.

Long before white settlers from Tennessee, Kentucky, and Alabama arrived at Petit Jean Mountain and established a settlement at the top, the local Indians knew about the ghost. As the newcomers worked hard to earn their living from cutting timber and farming the fertile soils found at the top, they often paused to visit with the few Indians who resided nearby. Fascinated, the settlers listened intently to the tales of the ghost.

The ghost, or spirit, as the Indians called it, was that of a lost and lonely young woman whose hope and dream of love was never fulfilled.

Sometime during the eighteenth century, according to the writings of the late T.W. Hardison, the French nobleman Rene Chauvet left his homeland in Europe to explore a portion of the Louisiana Territory to determine its suitability for trapping, trade, and French settlement.

With the full support of the King of France, Chauvet began making preparations to sail across the Atlantic to the New World. Before leaving, he met briefly with his betrothed, a beautiful young Parisian girl named Adrienne who was completely devoted to Chauvet. She begged to accompany her fiance, but Chauvet, fearful of the dangers and hardships likely to be encountered along the way, refused her pleadings. He told her that if he found the country across the sea to his liking, he would return for her and take her back as his wife. Kissing Adrienne tenderly, Chauvet bade the brokenhearted girl goodbye.

Adrienne, a spirited and adventurous lass, was not to be denied. She devised a cunning plan to travel to America with her beloved Chauvet. She cut her hair quite short, dressed herself in a man's clothes, and otherwise disguised herself to look like a boy. As Chauvet's ship was tied in port and being loaded with supplies, Adrienne approached one of the officers, said her name was Jean, and asked for a job as a cabin boy. She was immediately hired and put to work. This rather devious scheme enabled her to be near Chauvet, yet pass unknown among the crewmen and deckhands. The ship's crew took to calling her Petit Jean-Little John.

During the crossing of the Atlantic Ocean, Adrienne, in the course of her duties, came close to Chauvet many times, but because of her clever and effective disguise, the Frenchman never recognized her.

Following an uneventful crossing of the great sea and a portion of the Gulf of Mexico, Chauvet's ship finally entered the Mississippi River and sailed upstream. On reaching the confluence of the Arkansas River, Chauvet steered into it. Several days later, came to the foot of a mountain on the south side of the river, a low, vertical escarpment that rose from the surrounding valley, a picturesque low, elongated, wooded mountain topped with a dense oak-hickory forest that beckoned to the sailors.

A number of Indians gathered along the river bank at the foot of the mountain to greet the ship and its passengers. After welcoming the Frenchmen, the friendly natives invited Chauvet and his crew to climb to the top of the mountain and participate in a great feast. Chauvet was so enchanted with the cool, tree-covered mountaintop and with the Indians that he decided to spend the remainder of the summer here and ordered the construction of four permanent dwellings out of logs and stone.

On several occasions, Adrienne attempted to reveal her true identity to Chauvet, but each time she came near him she feared he would become angry with her and send her away. Throughout the summer, she helped the other crewmen hunt, fish, and construct cabins. As she went about her duties she watched Chauvet and longed to run to him, to hold him in her arms and to have him hold her. During the evenings following dinner, she kept to herself, eschewing the company of the crew. At night, she dreamed of Chauvet.

For his part, Chauvet thought often of Adrienne and wondered what she might be doing at that particular time back in France. He longed for her, ached for her, and counted the days until the time he would be able to return to his homeland and hold her in his arms.

As the autumn season approached, Chauvet announced they would soon be returning to France, and preparations were made for the long journey. For two full days, the sailors carried supplies and belongings down the steep mountain trail to the riverbank and loaded them onto the ship. On the evening before departure, however, Petit Jean fell ill, and was confined to her bed with high fever and convulsions. In her delirium, she called out for Chauvet.

When the explorer arrived at her bedside, the girl revealed to him her true identity. Stunned, Chauvet gathered Adrienne in his arms and expressed his deep love for her. Ordering the construction of a litter, he had her carried to the ship where she was placed in the more comfortable quarters of the captain's cabin. For days, Chauvet ministered to her and remained by her bedside. As he cared for his beloved, he prayed for her recovery.

It was not to be. One evening, Adrienne opened her eyes and saw Chauvet on his knees next to her bed, his hands holding hers. She reached out for him and told him that she feared she would never live to see France again. She asked that she be taken back to the mountaintop to spend her final days. Taking her in his strong arms, Chauvet gently carried her back up the mountain and placed her in one of the cabins. All night long he remained with her, bathing her fevered brow with cold rags. The following morning, however, Petit Jean was dead.

Chauvet buried Petit Jean near the eastern end of the mountain in a plot overlooking the ship that floated quietly on the river below. He mourned at her graveside for two days and nights. He cried until he had no more tears to shed. Finally, standing over the lonely grave, he kissed the crude marker placed atop it and bade her a choked and sobbing goodbye. With heavy heart, Rene Chauvet descended the mountain and joined his companions on the ship. The next morning, the Frenchmen sailed away, never to return.

For years afterward, the Indians claimed they often saw the ghost of Petit Jean walking along the edge of the mountain. Each time she appeared, she was always staring at the river below as if expecting someone to arrive.

In time, this beautiful mountain was named after Petit Jean, and during the 1900s it became a state park.

The earliest visitors to Petit Jean State Park were often surprised at spotting a ghost-like image hovering and moving around along the eastern escarpment. Observers always said the ghost was that of a young woman, and that she always seemed to be staring down the steep slope toward the landing on the Arkansas River near the base of the mountain. They all claimed it appeared as though she were looking for something, or someone.

The Ghost of the Rebel Sentinel

The Shepherd of the Hills theme park is located west of Branson, Missouri, in Taney County. This park is unique in that it has its own ghost, one that has been seen by hundreds of people over the years, and one whose consistent appearance continues to mystify employees and visitors alike.

A short distance west of Branson in the Missouri Ozarks lays Inspiration Point. This high altitude setting on an elongated limestone ridge provides the visitor with a wide and distant view of the surrounding countryside.

During the Civil War, Inspiration Point was an uninhabited, wooded ridge that played an important role in the movements of Rebel troops. The Confederates kept a sentinel posted atop Inspiration Point to keep a lookout for advancing Yankees. The sentinel, who sometimes remained on watch for several days at a time, was provided a horse, arms and ammunition, and sufficient rations. When the enemy was spotted, the sentinel would quickly saddle his horse and ride to the nearby encampments, alerting one and all to the approaching Federals.

During a certain period of the War, the sentinel assigned to Inspiration Point was surprised by Yankee scouts and killed before he could get away. His body was deposited in a wide crevice which, in turn, was filled with rocks. His comrades never learned of his fate.

Following the War, a few attempts were made to establish a settlement on the point, but the topsoil was too thin and poor, making it difficult to grow crops. The few families that tried and failed simply moved back down to the richer bottomlands. They returned to the cooler altitudes of Inspiration Point from time to time for picnics, family gatherings, and reunions.

During those years residents were attempting to establish homesteads in the area, several of them reported witnessing the appearance of a strange ghost. The apparition, a man on horseback and dressed in a Confederate uniform, was often seen riding through the woods and along the edge of the ridge. From time to time, the ghost was reported to have stopped and regarded the settlers, but after a few minutes turned and rode away.

During the 1870s, two of the settlers took time away from their crops to go deer hunting in the forest that covered much of the ridge. As they rode along an old game trail, the two men were suddenly and surprisingly joined by the ghost sentinel on horseback. Speechless with fright, the two hunters rode along for nearly one hundred yards with the ghost only a few feet away. As suddenly as it appeared, the apparition vanished.

During the time the Shepherd of the Hills theme park was being constructed, as well as for the years following as it grew in popularity, the ghost sentinel was often seen by workers and visitors alike. In fact, the ghost appeared so often one summer that employees got used to it such that they barely paid it much notice. Many even greeted the ghost with a wave each morning as they arrived for work and went about their chores.

While its numerous appearances have frightened many people, the ghost sentinel has never harmed anyone. To this day, the strange ghost is still seen by visitors to the park, but why it continues to appear has never been explained.

Mount Holly Cemetery Ghost

For years, Arkansas residents living near Little Rock's Mount Holly Cemetery have seen what appears to be a ghost horseman riding past the old gate on Little Rock's Arch Street. The ghost is believed to be that of Robert Kincaid, a member of a prominent Little Rock family who was murdered long ago while traveling along the road to Hot Springs.

Though the ghost horseman had been reported a number of times during the past several decades, very few Little Rock citizens were aware of the phenomenon until a newspaper reporter discovered an early reference to it in a personal journal maintained by the late Judge Samuel W. Williams. Williams, a well-known and highly respected jurist, actually saw the ghost himself. The reporter decided to write an article about the strange spirit for an Arkansas newspaper, thus alerting thousands to the presence of the spirit. Judge Williams, however, may have been the first person to actually view the apparition.

On the day before Williams saw the ghost, a Saturday, Robert Kincaid departed Little Rock on horseback, bound for Hot Springs on a business trip. Hot Springs is located approximately fifty-five miles to the southwest of Little Rock. Robert, who was the brother of Judge Williams' good friend and neighbor Charles Kincaid, rode a sorrel and wore a brown suit with a blue shirt and a brown derby hat. Somewhere near the town of Benton, Kincaid was ambushed by a farmer named Haws Ewan, who shot and killed both Kincaid and the horse. The reason for the killing was never determined, though it is believed that two men had a falling out over a business deal. Robert Kincaid's body lay on the ground next to the Little Rock-Hot Springs Road for twenty-four hours before he was discovered by the driver of a mail coach.

The next day following Sunday lunch, Judge Williams, along with his wife and daughter, went for their customary walk. Their route took them to the Mount Holly Cemetery into which they wandered, reading the names on the headstones. Several of Williams' former acquaintances were buried here, as were a number of important Arkansas historical figures, and it pleased the judge to relive the past and recall pleasant memories in this peaceful environment.

As Judge Williams and his family walked toward Eleventh Street from the cemetery, they were startled by the sudden appearance of a man on horseback riding at breakneck speed down Arch Street. Approaching the three, the rider reined up the sorrel several yards away and looked squarely at Williams. The judge immediately recognized the mounted horseman as Robert Kincaid, even noting that he was wearing a brown suit and derby hat. As the judge was about to call out a greeting, both man and horse suddenly vanished

Judge Williams turned toward his wife and said, "My God, that was Robert Kincaid!"

By now several others who were walking nearby ran over to where the judge stood and asked him what had just happened. They had all seen the horseman, and several in the crowd also recognized Kincaid. All were at a loss to explain the sudden disappearance.

Stunned by what he had seen, Williams hurried to the home of Charles Kincaid. After being received by his neighbor, Williams immediately asked his friend where Robert was. At the time, both men were unaware Robert had been killed, and Kincaid told Williams that his brother had gone to Hot Springs. Williams then asked Kincaid what Robert was wearing and he replied, "A brown suit and derby."

After Judge Williams explained what he, along with several other citizens, had just experienced at the Mount Holly Cemetery, Charles Kincaid assured his friend that it must have been a mistake, for Charles was not even in Little Rock.

The next morning as Judge Williams and Charles were drinking coffee on Kincaid's front porch, a messenger rode up with the news that Robert Kincaid had been killed on the road to Hot Springs two days earlier!

For years thereafter, the ghost of Robert Kincaid, wearing a brown suit, blue shirt, and brown derby, was seen on dozens of occasions riding a ghost sorrel down Arch Street.

The Ghosts of Happy Bend

In Conway County not far from the tree-lined banks of Point Remove Creek lies the small community of Happy Bend. Today, Happy Bend is a ghost town—in more ways than one. Virtually nothing is left of the once-thriving settlement, and the area is now primarily given over to farming, with a few residences here and there scattered among the tilled fields. Prior to the Civil War, however, Happy Bend was once an important stop for west-bound travelers and an occasional gathering place for prominent politicians and farmers.

Near the banks of Point Remove Creek and along the wide, farmed floodplain that separates the stream from the long-gone settlement of Happy Bend, strange spirits are sometimes seen moving about on moonlit nights—misty, ghostly images that appear to flit and dart among the trees and across the fertile bottomland. One observer stated that the spirits appear to be searching for something. Some say they can even hear the ghosts moaning.

The apparitions, it has been related by some old-timers, are believed to be the spirits of a number of victims who were brutally murdered, dismembered, and thrown into the creek by one W.O. Wilson, the owner of the Happy Bend's Wilson Hotel. For a time, the hotel and tavern were popular stopping places for stagecoaches and solitary travelers, and Wilson entertained any and all with stories, whiskey and, some said, even gambling and women.

For a few travelers, however, the Wilson Hotel was their final stop. Many a businessman who carelessly flashed his money around the Wilson Hotel was never seen again, and it was believed by area residents that the spirits seen wandering the floodplain sometimes at night belong to those unfortunate souls who met their end there.

W.O. Wilson was born and reared in Alabama in the foothills of the Appalachian Mountains. As a youth, he was chased out of his hometown for stealing from a merchant. He was also suspected of stealing a valuable racehorse, but the charge was finally dropped for lack of evidence. During the next decade, Wilson traveled throughout Missouri, Kansas, and Indian Territory, earning a reputation as a horse thief, gambler, and even a murderer who loved to brawl. Wilson was known as a hard drinker and a skilled fighter and would sometimes challenge two or three men at the same time, often beating them both badly. Though it was never proven, it is believed Wilson killed a lawman in Missouri before fleeing to Arkansas.

Wilson was indeed an intimidating figure, sporting a thick neck, broad shoulders, and big, bushy eyebrows that met above his nose. He had the sinewy, muscled arms and strong wide hands of a blacksmith, but dressed like a dandy. He always wore a black frock coat with tails and a black derby hat, his long black hair flowing freely behind.

After arriving in central Arkansas, Wilson purchased a parcel of land at Happy Bend not far from a pronounced curve of Point Remove Creek. Aware of the growing traffic between Little Rock and Fort Smith, Wilson decided to capitalize on it by constructing a two-story, eight room hotel. In spite of his threatening appearance, Wilson always managed to be a charming and entertaining host.

Not long after the opening of the hotel, strange stories began circulating throughout the area about travelers checking in and never being seen again. When confronted by his neighbors about these suspicions, Wilson always remained pleasant, and even invited an inspection of his property. Nothing was ever found that suggested wrongdoing.

One day, an influential businessman named William Paschal checked into the hotel and was never seen again. When Paschal's disappearance was finally reported, lawmen were called in, and, with the aid of dogs, searched the premises and the surrounding property. A dead horse, identified as belonging to Pashal, was found tied in a thicket not far from the creek, and Wilson, along with a slave woman who cooked and cleaned for him at the hotel, was arrested on suspicion of murder. Wilson remained charming and helpful during interrogation, even escorting the investigators around the grounds, but the black woman remained very nervous. She appeared terrified, more of Wilson than of the lawmen.

Unimpressed with Wilson's charm, however, the lawmen incarcerated him in the county jail on suspicion of murder. The slave woman was placed in a separate cell. Things were not looking good for the hotel owner.

On the second night after he was arrested, Wilson attacked a guard, knocking him unconscious, and escaped from the jail. He slipped down to the nearby bank of the Arkansas River, stole a boat, and rowed out to the middle of the river to catch the current. Wilson had no sooner pushed off from shore when two deputies arrived in pursuit, opened fire, and shot the fugitive, killing him. A moment later as the limp form of the prisoner slumped to the bottom of the boat, the deputies launched another craft, overtook Wilson, and returned with the body.

The next day, the slave woman expressed great relief on learning of the death of her master, and told the lawmen an incredible story. She revealed the existence of a trap door in the floor of one of the hotel rooms, a door that led to a deep underground cellar. The woman claimed Wilson would club an unsuspecting guest with a heavy mallet and drag the limp form to this cellar. There, the victim would be stripped of all valuables, including guns, gold teeth, and even boots. Wilson would then hack the victim to pieces with a meat cleaver, place the parts in weighted sacks, and order the woman to drag them to Point Remove Creek and throw them into the stream. When she returned from that grisly task, she was required to clean up the blood from the most recent butchering.

Several days later when Happy Bend residents learned of the hotel owner's grisly activities, they immediately set fire to the Wilson Hotel and burned it to the ground, determined to remove Wilson's legacy forever.

But it was not to be, because a short time after the hotel burned down, the ghosts of what many believed to be Wilson's victims were often seen gliding along the banks of Point Remove Creek and the nearby floodplain. For the most part, the ghosts appeared to be those of men, but some claimed to have seen a woman on occasion. Most of the ghosts, it was reported, were headless.

W.O. Wilson is buried in the old cemetery at what used to be the town of Lewisburg. Today, there is no trace of his hotel in Happy Bend. Every now and then, however, someone—a deer hunter or a farmer—will spot the ghosts in the evening just after sundown, silent spirits floating just above the ground among the trees that line the bank of the creek.

The ghosts of Happy Bend are still seen today. Some say they are looking for Wilson to exact revenge on the murderer. Others claim they are searching for their valuables which are believed to be buried somewhere nearby. A few believe they are looking for their missing heads.

Others maintain that the ghosts are there simply to remind us of the evil that men do.

The Haunted Headstone

Southwest City, Missouri, as the name implies, is located in the extreme southwestern tip of the state in McDonald County where it joins with Arkansas and Oklahoma. This small community of some six hundred souls claims one of the strangest hauntings ever to be recorded in the annals of graveyard spirits. The location of this bizarre phenomenon is a tiny cemetery located nearby, and the strange and incredible occurrence that has transpired there continues to baffle investigators and remains an impenetrable mystery today. As a result of what has been discovered there, some nearby residents refuse to set foot in the cemetery.

In this relatively small and simple cemetery can be found a variety of headstones—some of them are quite plain, some are a bit more ornate, and many of them are quite old, having served this area for well over one hundred years. An intricately carved statue of a woman can be found on one of the headstones that could possibly be an angel. While she appears angelic, she possesses no wings. That, in itself, is not unusual, but, according to those who have witnessed it, the figure changes positions in spite of the fact that it is carved from solid marble!

The story of the strange headstone in the Southwest City, Missouri, cemetery came to light during the 1960s. Amazingly, the discovery that the headstone was haunted took place in Denver, Colorado.

In 1964, a number of families with strong Ozark ties were participating in a reunion at a downtown Denver hotel. The gathering lasted for two days and was rich with reminiscences, re-acquaintances, and renewals of old friendships.

To acquaint some of the younger relatives and those who grew up in other parts of the country who were not familiar with their Ozark homeland, several of the women brought albums filled with pictures of the community, the downtown area, churches, the surrounding landscape, several kinfolks, and the cemetery. During the course of the gathering, a small group of Southwest City residents announced to all assembled that they were taking up a collection of money to send back home to be used for the care and maintenance of the cemetery, wherein were buried a number of deceased relatives of those in attendance.

One of the women produced a photograph of one particular headstone. It consisted of a stout and handsome marble base containing all of the appropriate inscription and was topped by a finely sculpted statue, also marble, of a female figure. The woman identified it as the marker for her aunt's grave, commented on the beauty of the sculpture, and passed it around for all to see.

Another woman, a cousin to the first, also recalled the fine marker, and, after searching through her own photograph album, produced another picture of the same headstone and handed it to those gathered around.

After a number of people had examined the photographs, one of the men gasped in astonishment. Calling everyone around him, he pointed to the two separate photographs of the marker. In each photograph, the name of the deceased, along with the dates of birth and death, were clearly inscribed and readable on the base. In one of the photographs, the statue of the female figure was in a kneeling position, head bowed, and hands clasped as in prayer. The second photograph, however, showed the exact same marker but the statue was holding its arms outstretched and the head was raised as if looking toward the heavens.

No one at the gathering could explain the incredible differences in the postures of what apparently was the same stone statue. Finally, one of the Southwest City residents said she would go to the cemetery on returning home and solve the mystery once and for all.

Two weeks later, the woman drove the short distance from her house to the cemetery and located the statue. There, before her, was the marker with the statue atop it, the same marker that was evident in the two photographs examined in Denver. Examining the statue, she noted that it was clearly in a kneeling position, head bowed, and hands clasped in front. At the first opportunity, she promised herself, she would return with her camera, take a photograph and mail copies to all of those who were confused about the statue.

Various obligations and chores kept the woman from returning immediately, but two weeks later she woman drove to the cemetery with her camera and walked directly to the statue. This time, she received the shock of her life when she noticed that the stone figure was not kneeling, but was standing with its arms outstretched to its sides and the head looking directly forward. Panicked, the woman dropped her camera and fled from the cemetery, never to return.

Besides those certain Southwest City, Missouri, families and relatives—all of whom wish to remain anonymous and refuse to discuss the subject any longer—very few people are aware of the curious statue in the nearby cemetery. Some skeptical observers claim the story of the marble statue that changes positions is nothing more than a hoax. The photographs, however, do not lie, and clearly reveal different positions for the figure.

The relatives of the deceased who is covered by the marker refuse to speak to anyone and it is uncertain if they are aware of some reason why the headstone would be haunted. An investigation into the life of the relative buried beneath the marker provides no information pertinent to the haunting. Efforts to learn the identity of the artisan who carved the image of the woman on the headstone likewise have met with failure.

The mystery is yet to be explained.

Ghost Plane near Berryville

Two evenings prior to Halloween in 1975, a violent thunderstorm rocked the Ozark Mountains just north of the Carroll County town of Berryville in Arkansas. The extremely high winds, accompanied by violent lightning and heavy rainfall, left three persons dead, tore the roofs from several dwellings, barns, and chicken houses, and uprooted dozens of trees, some of them over one hundred years old. Estimates of the damage exceeded one million dollars.

During the height of the thunderstorm, several Carroll County residents claimed that above the din of thunder and lightning they heard the droning sound of an airplane, a noise followed only seconds later by the unmistakable sound of an explosion in the distance.

The next day as Berryville residents surveyed the storm damage, Roy Littrell was standing in his front yard when he noticed a large piece of twisted aluminum lying near the edge of his property. Closer inspection revealed it had been part of an airplane.

About the same time in another part of town, Mike Gallagher discovered more airplane wreckage. An hour later even more pieces of metal, all apparently from a plane, were found east of town. After inspecting the damaged debris, authorities concluded the following day that they all came from a twin-engine Cessna Golden Eagle. The scattered pieces of twisted wreckage suggested the plane might have exploded. Some advanced the notion it may have been struck by lightning. The next morning, an air search for what remained of the plane was launched.

Around sundown, a search plane spotted the wreckage of the Cessna in the rocky and rugged limestone bluffs near the Kings River, about five miles south of town and close to a location known locally as Trigger Gap. By the time the ground search party arrived at the site, it was dark. Using flashlights and torches, they continued to work throughout the night, investigating the damaged aircraft.

At the outset, all involved agreed it was one of the strangest airplane crashes anyone had ever seen. Hundreds of pieces of the twisted metal from the craft, small and large, were found scattered across a twenty-mile-wide area, but the fuselage was completely intact. Both doors and the wings had been violently ripped off, but evidence suggested the body of the plane apparently dropped straight down out of the sky—there was virtually no damaged timber around the wreck as normally occurs when a disabled craft glides to a forced landing.

The investigation also revealed no evidence of an explosion or even a fire. Oddly, the plane's fire extinguisher, discovered about a quarter mile from the fuselage, had obviously been used, but for what purpose no one knows.

The most gruesome discovery was from inside the airplane—three dead bodies, each of them carrying identification showing they were residents of Colorado.

Investigative work by local law enforcement authorities and the Federal Aeronautics Administration revealed that the plane was transporting a briefcase filled with $20,000 in cash, supposedly part of a payroll being delivered to a mining operation in Paducah, Kentucky. No sign of the briefcase or money, however, was ever found.

Curiously, rumors of a fourth passenger surfaced during the investigation, but authorities studying the accident refused to provide any pertinent information.

The mysterious plane crash of 1975 has perplexed Carroll County residents for years. The Federal Aeronautics Administration that monitored the investigation never offered an explanation relative to the strange manner in which the plane had broken up, and no one has ever come forward with information pertaining to why the aircraft was so far off the established flight path between Denver and Paducah. Inquiries addressed to the investigating officials were met with stony silences.

When word of the missing $20,000 was leaked, a number of area residents hiked into the Trigger Gap area in search of it. Additionally, professional and amateur treasure hunters from as far away as California arrived in the area and conducted searches for the money, but to date it has never been found. What was encountered at the wreck site, however, was a ghost.

During the next several years, many of the treasure hunters who braved the rugged and rocky Ozark Mountain country along with the dense population of poisonous snakes in the woods south of Berryville have reported seeing a ghostly form moving around in the area of the crash site. The ghost appears to be searching for something, and most of those who are familiar with the facts concerning the airplane crash believe it is looking for the lost money. Many also believe the ghost is the spirit form of the rumored fourth passenger?

When the treasure hunters get within forty feet of the ghost, however, it disappears. Sometimes it remains invisible, and other times it appears moments later several yards away.

The supposed connection between the ghost and the missing money is indeed a conundrum. Why would a ghost search for money? And what if it found the $20,000? What would it do? A ghost certainly cannot spend money.

There was yet another mystery associated with the Carroll County plane crash. Each year, late in the evening two days before Halloween, rural Carroll County residents sometimes hear the ghostly sound of a low-flying airplane, a sound that is followed by another —an explosion. Subsequent investigation has never yielded any evidence whatsoever of another plane crash.

The Hardin Hill Haunting

In Faulkner County in east-central Arkansas at the intersection of the historical Springfield-Des Arc and Little Rock-Clinton roads lies Hardin Hill. To this day, travelers driving along the bladed road that passes between the hill and the East Fork of Cadron Creek sometimes report seeing the ghosts of people moving slowly along the stream bank as well as a portion of the adjacent floodplain between the creek and a small cemetery. As if encountering spirits in this remote portion of Faulkner County were not bad enough, the event is made doubly frightening, because the ghosts seen here are all headless.

According to some researchers, these specters may very well be the ghosts of people killed by Jonathan Hardin, a prominent resident of the area during the early part of the nineteenth century.

History records that Jonathan Hardin arrived in this region sometime during the 1820s. With the help of fifteen slaves, he farmed the fertile floodplain adjacent to the East Fork of the Cadron Creek, built a fine, large, two-story cabin, a blacksmith shop, slave quarters, and a stable.

Hardin's house was constructed atop a nearby hill—since named Hardin Hill—while the rest of the structures were built just south of the prominence near its base. Passing close to the lower slopes of Hardin Hill was the Little Rock-Clinton Road. While this area is now considered almost remote and isolated by some, it was a busy intersection up until the mid-1880s. Because the Little Rock-Clinton road saw a great deal of traffic in those days, Hardin's house also served as an inn for travelers.

A short time after Hardin moved into his new quarters and established a successful farming operation, he married Elizabeth Greathouse, a local widow with three children and the daughter of a prominent farmer who lived nearby.

During the next several years, according to legend, many travelers who checked into Hardin's inn were never seen again. Though it was never proven, local gossip maintained that Hardin killed them, took their valuables, and then dragged their bodies to an old abandoned graveyard located between the hill and the creek. Here, the stories say, the victims were buried. Before interring the corpses, however, Hardin reputedly severed the heads from the bodies and, swinging them by the hair, tossed them into the creek.

Despite oft-repeated suspicions voiced by several area residents, Hardin was never charged with any crimes. When the sheriff and deputies arrived at his Hardin Hill home to question him about the disappearances of some of his lodgers, Hardin greeted them cordially, shook hands all around, and even invited the lawmen to a fine dinner of roast duck, dried apple cobbler, homemade wine, and peach brandy.

Around this time, Hardin became a well-respected businessman and wielded a great deal of power and influence. It was widely rumored that Hardin's fortune helped elect the county sheriff, the very man who was investigating him.

It was also suggested that Hardin conducted a clandestine business purchasing stolen goods from robbers who preyed on travelers and settlers who lived in remote areas. Furthermore, it was common knowledge among several Faulkner County residents that Hardin's inn often served as a hideout for outlaws. In subsequent years, local lore maintained that Frank and Jesse James, as well as a number of other notorious badmen, were frequent visitors to the Hardin house.

Despite the rumors that he had murdered some of his guests and was involved in illegal activities, Jonathan Hardin eventually gained a reputation as a solid citizen and a contributing member of the community. He even served for a time as court magistrate, was known for miles around as a successful and prosperous businessman and farmer, and in 1852 donated ten acres of his farmland near the Holland community for a church site.

Hardin passed away in 1869 at the age of sixty-nine. He is buried in the old Hardin Hill Cemetery alongside his wife. Both gravesites have been vandalized over the years by treasure hunters who are convinced Hardin had a significant amount of his wealth buried with him in his casket.

Though no treasure has ever been found, the Hardin legend is kept alive today by the occasional appearance of the headless ghosts who are most often seen around dusk on moonlit nights near the old neglected and overgrown graveyard.

Alf Bolin's Ghost

Though not widely known, Alf Bolin was one of the most notorious outlaws of his time in the southwestern Missouri Ozark Mountains. In recent years, he has become one of the area's most famous ghosts.

During the Civil War, Bolin swore allegiance neither to the North nor the South. Instead, he organized a gang of some thirty or forty renegades, robbers, and murderers and terrorized settlers and military alike throughout much of Stone County, Missouri. It was once reported that the Alf Bolin gang was responsible for at least fifty murders.

So feared and dangerous was Bolin that the Union army offered a $5,000 reward for his capture or death. According to local lore, several men made attempts to capture or kill Bolin, but all met their own death at the hands of the renegade. It has also been told that those who tried to take Bolin's life were generally captured and subsequently subjected to horrible tortures before they were put to death. Their bodies were often hung from trees or nailed to the sides of barns as a warning to others who might try to collect the reward. By then, Bolin had deservedly earned the reputation of a madman.

Robert Foster, a Confederate sympathizer was finally instrumental in putting an end to Bolin's outlaw career. While a prisoner at the Union army camp at Springfield, Foster offered to capture or kill Bolin in exchange for his freedom. Foster explained Bolin could be lured to his cabin, only a short distance from the outlaw's hideout. Once there, Foster felt certain Bolin could be apprehended.

Intrigued with the plan, Federal officials agreed to implement it but without the help of Foster. Instead, they sent Corporal Z.E. Thomas of the Iowa Volunteer Cavalry to carry out Foster's plan.

Thomas traveled to the Foster cabin and even moved into it with Bolin's wife. According to the plan, Mrs. Foster invited Bolin to the residence ostensibly to sell him some cattle. Bolin arrived several days later and was introduced to Thomas, who was identified as a Confederate soldier who had escaped from a Union prison.

During the visit, Bolin turned to light his pipe. While the outlaw's attention was distracted, Thomas struck him solidly in the back of the head with a plow handle and knocked him unconscious. Thomas, however, was convinced Bolin was dead and dragged the limp form into the barn and covered it with hay. As Thomas busied himself with saddling his horse, Bolin regained consciousness, threw off a portion of his covering of hay, and attempted to stand. Hearing the commotion, Thomas turned, drew his cap and ball pistol, and shot a bullet through the heart of the outlaw, ending his wicked life once and for all.

After finishing saddling his horse, Thomas left immediately for Union headquarters at Springfield. On the following day, he returned with a wagon and a contingent of twenty-five cavalrymen, and Bolin's corpse was thrown into the back of the wagon to be returned to Springfield.

While Thomas was leading the party back to headquarters, angry, revenge-minded residents of the town of Forsythe approached the wagon and, while Thomas was distracted, jumped into it and severed the dead outlaw's head from his body. After burying the headless corpse, Thomas placed Bolin's head in a gunnysack and, accompanied by the cavalrymen, continued on to Springfield. On reaching the town of Ozark in Christian County, however, another mob approached the wagon and seized the head. After mounting it on a long pole, they erected it on the courthouse lawn where they threw rocks at it all day long. When the head finally reached Springfield, it was little more than a battered skull covered with dry, stretched skin.

Shockingly, Bolin's activities did not end with his death, and there are a few old-timers still living in the Missouri Ozarks that claim his ghost still roams the countryside.

When Alf Bolin was killed and beheaded in 1863, Ozark residents breathed a collective sigh of relief. No longer would they be terrorized by this madman and his cutthroat companions. No longer would they be driven from their homes, robbed at gunpoint, and tortured.

Their relief was short-lived, however, for within weeks of the burial of his headless corpse in the town of Ozark, frightened citizens began reporting encounters with his ghost.

The spirit assumes two forms: One is the head, and the other is the headless body.

One night about two months following the beheading of Alf Bolin, a livery operator was walking home from his place of business, his route taking him past the courthouse where the severed head of Bolin had served as a target for angry, rock-throwing citizens.

As he passed the courthouse, the liveryman heard a low moan, a sound suggesting someone was in extreme pain. Peering through the darkness, he looked toward the courthouse square from which the sound emanated, but he could see nothing. As he searched for the source of the strange noise, it came again, this time from a level about ten feet above the ground. Glancing upward, the liveryman gazed in terror at the shriveled and bloodied head and face of Alf Bolin hovering in the approximate spot where it had been mounted on a pole weeks earlier. Turning away from the grisly sight, the liveryman fled to his home and told his wife what he had seen.

That same night, at least three others saw the ghostly head, seemingly floating in the darkness above the courthouse square. Word of the apparition soon spread throughout the area, and nightly dozens of the curious gathered at the edge of the grassy area to gaze upon the unnerving sight of Alf Bolin's head, an image that remained visible for only a few seconds at a time, moaning and screaming all the while.

Several months following the appearance of the ghost head, a second frightening form was seen. Near the location of Alf Bolin's burial site, an apparition was seen walking throughout the area as if searching for something. On closer inspection, observers discovered the shadowy figure was headless. Night after night the form appeared, and area citizens grew convinced it was Alf Bolin's headless body roaming the region in search of the severed head.

Over the years, both the head and the headless body were occasionally seen at night by hundreds of eyewitnesses until around the 1930s when the appearances grew fewer and fewer. By the 1940s, say old-timers who still live in the area, hardly anyone reported seeing either the head or the body.

Most of those who witnessed the ghostly appearances are long gone now, and the tales of the bizarre hauntings are, for the most part, just a dim memory among very few. Once in a great while though, someone walking by the old courthouse late at night will hear a low, moaning sound coming from somewhere above the ground, as if from the trees.

Alf Bolin's ghost, while not as active as it was in the past, is, according to some of those who claim to know, still lurking in the Ozark darkness.

The Haunted Grave

Not far from the town of Doniphan, Ripley County, Missouri, is a small, old cemetery which contains a cluster of weathered headstones amid a grassy lawn that has gone untended for many years. Near one end of this abandoned graveyard is a cherry tree, one that has grown out of the head of one of the graves. Several decades ago, this cherry tree figured significantly in the deaths of three prominent area residents.

During the 1920s, a poor man named James Barker lived in the alleys and under porches around Doniphan's business district. (Some accounts provide other first names for this individual, including Frank, John, and Simon, as well as different surnames including Barton and Baker).

The unfortunate Barker would have been considered a homeless person today. To fight off the misery of depression and poverty, Barker stayed drunk most of the time. Some claim he was miserable and depressed because of the liquor. Though Barker occasionally sought employment, he remained somewhat satisfied with begging for handouts from sympathetic citizens.

Barker tried several times to land a job at the town's largest grocery store, but the owner, a severe man who possessed neither tolerance nor compassion, discouraged his attempts. The owner did not care at all for Barker's seedy, unkempt, and ragged appearance, and each time the poor man entered the store, the owner would summon the police and have him escorted out into the street. Ordinarily, Barker was in the store only long enough to grab a handful of fresh cherries out of one of the bins and stuff them into his pocket.

Once, after Barker was thrown out of the grocery store, he wandered into a nearby hardware emporium and asked the proprietor for a job. As he spoke, Barker popped cherries into his mouth, chewed off the tasty fruit, and spit the seeds onto the wooden floor of the establishment. On seeing this, the owner of the hardware store grabbed an axe handle and chased him away, beating him across the shoulders as he ran. Out in the street, the owner pushed Barker to the ground, held the end of the axe handle against his throat, and, in front of several witnesses, threatened to kill him if he ever entered the hardware store again.

Picking himself up off the ground, Barker tried to maintain some sense of dignity as he brushed the dirt from his ragged coat. Looking directly at the merchant, Barker told him he would regret embarrassing him. Barker turned and walked away down the street, pulling cherries from his coat and popping them into his mouth.

On yet another occasion, Barker tried to secure a job at the railroad depot. The manager, knowing, Barker's weakness for liquor, rudely turned him away, chastising him for his drinking in front of a group of passengers who were waiting for a train. The depot manager loudly scorned Barker as a drunkard and a bum. Reddening, Barker told the manager he would be sorry for treating him in this manner. Then, humiliated, Barker slunk away past the staring passengers.

Several weeks later, after being chased out of the grocery store once again, Frank Barker, his pockets filled with fresh cherries, walked down the main street of town, gleefully eating the delicious cherries one by one. Presently, he stopped, grabbed his throat, and fell to the ground, writhing violently and apparently finding it hard to breathe. Moments later, Frank Barker was dead. The town's mortician, who gave him a cursory examination, discovered a large cherry pit had lodged in Barker's throat, causing him to choke to death. The mortician decided not to attempt to remove the cherry pit and left it where he found it.

James Barker was given a pauper's burial at one end of the old cemetery located about two miles from town. A small, simple headstone marked the grave. Inscribed on the marker was only his name—James Barker, and the date of his death.

Several weeks following Barker's interment, a sapling sprouted from the ground just in front of the headstone, approximately where the head of the deceased would have been located. It was identified as a cherry tree. Since this little cemetery went untended for long periods of time, no one bothered to remove the tree.

As time passed, the cherry tree grew. Long, stout, healthy limbs branched out, eventually shading Barker's plot. Those few who passed through this region and noticed the tree remarked that it seemed to grow rapidly and that it matured much earlier than most cherry trees.

One morning, about ten years after the death of Frank Barker, the owner of the grocery store failed to show up for work one morning. For nearly a full day the town was searched but he could not be found. Sometime during the early evening, a farmer drove his wagon into town to report that he found a dead man hanging by a noose from a cherry tree which grew in a small, abandoned graveyard some distance away. The dead man, he said, was dangling just above the grave of someone named James Barker, according to the headstone. On investigation, the town's police chief discovered the hanged man was the grocer! According to the grocer's wife, the deceased admitted he had experienced terrible dreams about James Barker the previous night, was unable to eat breakfast, and left the house in a very agitated state of mind.

Nearly one year later to the day, the owner of the hardware store told his employees he had several nightmares concerning James Barker and experienced some difficulty sleeping. A short time after opening his store, he removed his apron, told his workers that he wasn't feeling well, and that he was going out for a few minutes to get some fresh air. It was the last time they saw him alive.

When the owner had not returned by closing time, one of the employees summoned the police. The next morning, the owner was found lying dead in the small graveyard out of town, stretched out across the grave of James Barker and directly under the cherry tree. He had apparently suffered a fatal heart attack.

Six months following the death of the hardware merchant, the manager of the railroad depot rose from a disturbed slumber one night and told his wife he couldn't sleep, that he was going for a walk to try to relax. When he failed to return by dawn, the worried wife called the police. Later that same day, the body of the depot manager was found lying atop James Barker's grave. He had apparently climbed the cherry tree, fallen, and suffered a broken back on impact with the ground.

For years afterward, it was whispered around the Ripley County area that James Barker—the poor, destitute bum who wandered the streets of Doniphan—had somehow reached beyond the grave to exact revenge on his tormentors. Other residents of the town who had been less than kind to the unfortunate Barker when he was alive now began to worry that his spirit may seek them out and provide the same revenge that had apparently claimed the others. One man who was known to be somewhat harsh with Barker was found dead one morning, the victim of an automobile accident. It seems that the man was driving home late one night from a business appointment in Poplar Bluff when his car left the road and slammed into a tree, killing the driver instantly.

Though the accident occurred several miles from the little abandoned cemetery in which James Barker had been buried many years ago, it was noted that the tree struck by the car was a cherry tree.

Coincidence? Some believe so, but many others are convinced that the spirit of James Barker had once again reached out from the grave to claim a victim.

Animal Ghosts

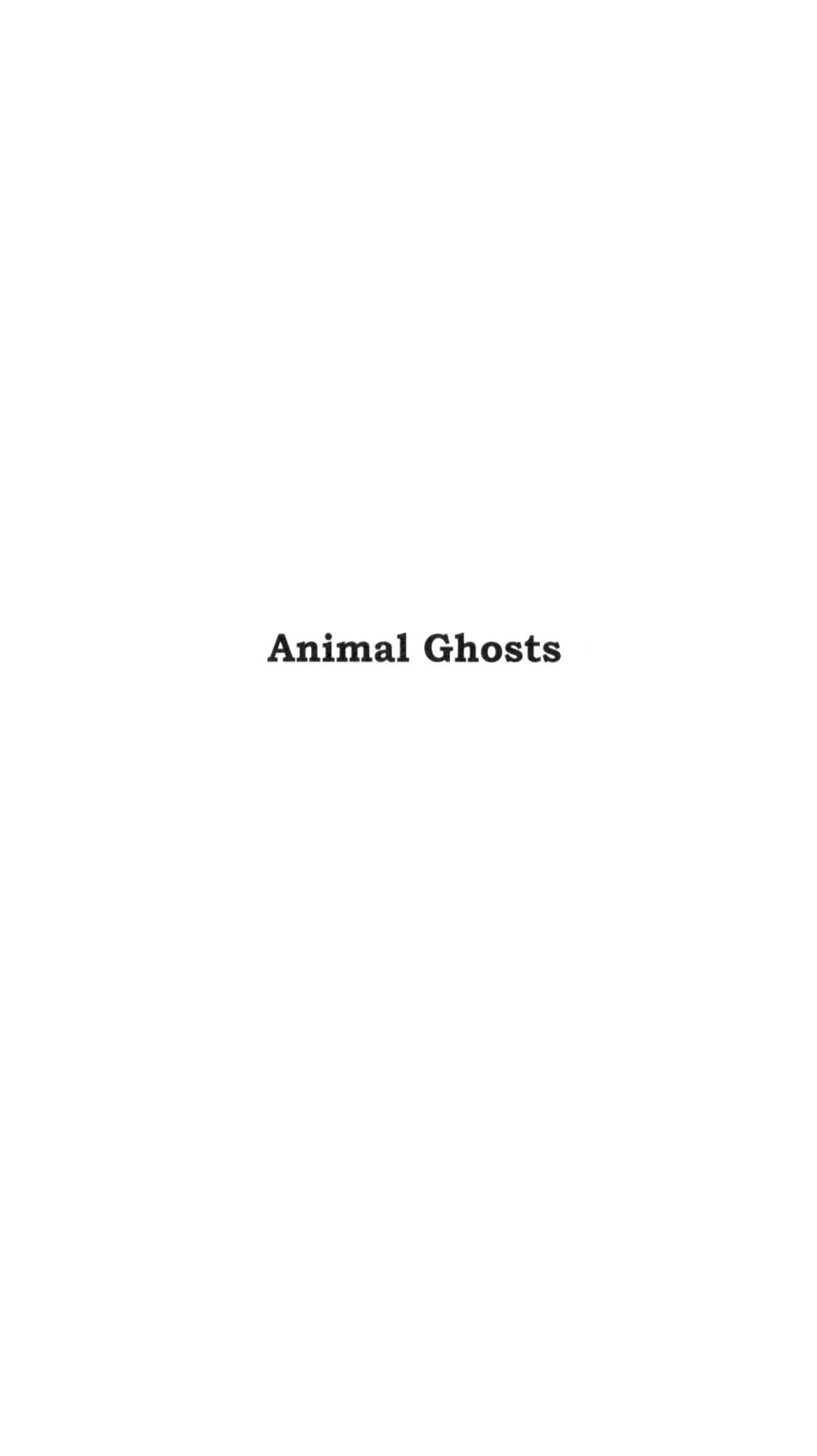

The Ghost Dog of Marion County

Milton Johnson was born and raised in the Arkansas Ozarks and lived most of his life in a stout log cabin built by his grandfather in 1908. Johnson, a cattle farmer, was well-known and well-liked by many in the Marion County area as a talented banjo and dulcimer player who regularly performed at fairs and reunions and sang many of the old-time folk ballads. Johnson, just like his father before him, entertained several generations of Marion County residents. Johnson was a widower, and had lived alone on his farm for about fifteen years.

One day during the 1970s, a Fayetteville, Arkansas, newspaper reporter telephoned Johnson and asked if he could come to his house to interview him for a feature article and take a few photographs. Johnson agreed and provided detailed directions to his remote Ozark home. He told the reporter to blow his car horn several times on arriving since he would likely be working somewhere out in his field or behind the house.

After leaving the blacktop and driving along four or five miles of bladed dirt and gravel road, the reporter finally arrived at an unlocked gate. After letting himself in and closing the gate behind him, he drove along the tree-lined lane and eventually pulled up in front of Johnson's log cabin. Before turning off the ignition, the reporter blew the horn three times, then climbed out of his car.

Johnson was nowhere to be seen, but from around the corner of the log cabin bounded a dog—a mid-size, golden-haired animal that appeared to be a cross between a retriever and a collie.

At first, the reporter feared he would be mistaken for a trespasser and was about to jump back into his car before he was bitten, but the dog proved to be only curious and quite friendly. He gave the newcomer a few cautious identifying sniffs, wagged his tail, and then raised a paw in a handshaking gesture. The reporter returned the shake.

Deciding that Johnson was probably occupied with some chore on another part of the farm, the reporter, accompanied by the dog, stepped up onto the front porch and sat down to wait in a wooden rocker. The companionable dog stretched out next to him, and the newspaperman occasionally reached down to scratch him behind one ear.

About thirty minutes later, the reporter was alerted to Johnson's arrival by a booming hello from an adjacent field. He could see the farmer walking toward him from where he had apparently been working. A few moments later, the wiry, blue denim-overalled, straw-hatted Johnson strode up, introduced himself, and invited the reporter into the house.

Once inside, Johnson excused himself to wash his hands and change into clean clothes and left the reporter to wander around the living room looking at the farmer's collection of musical instruments and old photographs hanging from the walls and resting on the mantel. Many of the photographs appeared to be of family members. On the mantel was a framed photo of the dog which greeted the reporter earlier, and as the guest was examining it, Johnson, dressed in a pressed pair of clean slacks, walked back into the room, drying his hands on a towel.

Johnson invited the reporter to have a seat, and for a while the two men talked about a variety of topics including farming, music, and family. As the reporter asked questions, the energetic farmer answered them as he paced back and forth across the spacious room.

During a lull in the interview, the reporter pointed to the picture of the dog on the mantelpiece and commented on how friendly he was and how he enjoyed his short visit with him on the porch. At the comment, Johnson suddenly stopped in mid-stride with a stunned look on his face and asked the visitor what he was talking about.

The reporter explained to his host about how the friendly dog had greeted him when he arrived, and how the two of them sat together in the shade of the porch while waiting for the farmer to show up.

Johnson, visibly shaken, walked over to the photo and stared at it for a long time. He told the reporter the dog's name was Bo, and that he found him alongside the blacktop many years ago when he was a puppy. It was only a few weeks after his wife passed away. Bo, he said, was the only company he'd had on the farm for a long time.

Johnson reminisced about sitting near the hearth with Bo on many a cold winter night, and of the dog accompanying him on long walks through the fields as he went about his chores. When Johnson played music, the dog would sit close by, watching and listening, and apparently enjoying himself. The dog, explained Johnson, traveled with him to folk festivals and other shows, and even became a favorite among the other singers, musicians, and performers.

Johnson took a deep breath and stood quietly looking out the living room window toward his field. The silence was broken only by the ticking of a large table clock. After a minute passed, the reporter commented that it must be nice to have a good dog like that around to keep one company.

Johnson, now with tears in his eyes, turned back toward the reporter and said this often happened when someone comes to visit. When the reporter asked what he meant, the farmer told him that what he saw was not a dog, but a ghost.

Presently, Johnson rose from his chair and walked back to the mantle piece. He picked up the framed picture, stared at it for several seconds, and after replacing it looked back at his guest.

Milton Johnson then told the reporter that Bo had died fifteen years earlier!

Phantom Black Panther Haunts Faulkner County

Since the 1940s, rural residents of central Arkansas' Faulkner County have occasionally reported sighting a mysterious black panther. The panther is normally seen near the shores of Lake Conway, but has been spotted as far as fifteen miles away near the northern boundary of the county where the rugged foothills of the Ozark Mountains likely offer more places to hide. The panther, believed by some to be a black-phase mountain lion, goes by many names: cougar, lion, painter, puma, and catamount. Some, however, refer to it as a ghost.

There are two extremely puzzling aspects to the reports of the black panther in this part of the Ozarks. First of all, biologists maintain that true black panthers and black-phase mountain lions simply do not exist in the United States. Though sightings of these apparently rare creatures have allegedly occurred throughout portions of Arkansas, Texas, and Florida, acceptable evidence in the form of a photograph or a trapped or killed specimen has never surfaced to support the contention that this animal actually lives here. A black panther-like creature called an onza, native to Mexico and Central America, is also extremely rare and has been seen by only a handful of people. In the United States, there are no verified reports of onzas.

Secondly, each time Faulkner County's black panther is approached, observers claim it vanishes into thin air after remaining visible for a short time!

While some insist that this black panther exists only in folklore and the imaginations of some men and women, a number of reputable citizens have admitted to seeing the cat, and have even claimed to have heard its screams.

Only a few instances of black panther encounters in the Ozark Mountains were officially recorded during the 1940s and 1950s. During the 1960s and 1970s, law enforcement agencies were occasionally called upon to investigate the growing number of reports of the mysterious cat that seemed to be lurking around Lake Conway.

Regarding the most recent reports, in virtually every case, one or more observers insisted they watched the black panther for several minutes at a time, but when they walked toward it, the animal disappeared. It never appeared menacing, it never attacked anyone, and it never ran away—it simply vanished into thin air. In the locations where the panther was seen, no tracks were ever found, even though the footprints of dogs and raccoons were visible.

In 1974, Henry Dobbs, who lived along the western shore of Faulkner County's Lake Conway, related that the screaming of a panther woke him up late one night. Concerned about his chickens, Dobbs hurriedly dressed, grabbed his rifle, and went outside to investigate. After inspecting his chicken coop and finding everything in order, he was about to return to the house when he spotted a black panther standing in his yard not thirty feet away. The moon was full, and the eyes of the cat, which Dobbs described as being very large, gleamed brightly. Dobbs immediately raised his rifle to fire at the cat, but the animal, he said, faded away right before his eyes, much like smoke disappears in a breeze.

Dobbs said he has seen the black panther on a number of other occasions over a period of approximately four years. Each sighting, he stated, lasted for no more than one or two minutes before the cat disappeared, leaving no trace whatsoever. Though it would have been an easy matter for the large black cat to kill Dobbs' chickens, none of them were ever harmed.

One of Dobbs' neighbors stated he had also seen the black cat many times, and on each occasion, it slowly faded from view after being visible for only a few seconds.

In 1988, the Arkansas State Game and Fish Commission hired world-famous lion tracker Roy McBride of Alpine, Texas, to conduct field investigations in the state. After spending several weeks in the area traveling thousands of miles and interviewing dozens of residents, McBride concluded that there were no suitable habitats for mountain lions in Arkansas. The lions spotted in the state, he suggested, were transients and not permanent residents.

Apparently McBride's deductions did not include ghosts, for since his visit, several more encounters with the black panther in Faulkner County have been reported.

One particularly curious incident occurred in 1993. An elderly woman who lived on Lake Conway's western shore saw the black panther late one evening while sitting on her porch swing. Rushing into her house, she grabbed her camera and returned outside. The black cat had not moved, and remained stationary as she walked up to it. The only movement, said the woman, was a slight twitching of the long, black tail. After stopping within twenty feet of the animal, she raised her camera and very slowly and deliberately took three photographs. The cat, she said, just sat quietly staring at her, occasionally blinking its "large yellow eyes." As she advanced the film on her camera following the third exposure, the cat suddenly vanished. She said she had only looked away for a second or two and when she looked up to take another photograph, the cat was gone. It made no sound—it simply disappeared.

Three days later when the woman picked up her developed photographs, the entire roll of film produced clear pictures except for the three photos she took of the black panther. In those three photographs, she stated, all that was apparent was a cloudy mist where the cat should have been.

Why the ghostly black panther prefers to haunt the environs of Lake Conway is not known. Though a mountain lion may live up to twenty years in the wild, the Faulkner County black panther has been observed by residents for over fifty years.

The Ghost Wolf

An elusive and mysterious white timber wolf roams throughout a portion of the Ozark foothills in southwestern Cleburne County, Arkansas, not far from Greers Ferry Lake and the small town of Quitman. This strange canine apparition has been seen and heard for decades, and as population growth and recreational activities increased in that part of the state, sightings grew more and more frequent. As they increased, so did the mystery surrounding the strange phenomena.

Farmers and other residents near the town of Quitman have made numerous unsuccessful attempts to shoot and trap the wolf over the years, but like the spirit it appears to be, it simply fades away only to reappear moments later at some distance. According to those who claimed to have seen it, the wolf materialized as a translucent white form only during bright moonlit nights. The ghost wolf has been described as "floating" across the landscape and radiating narrow, foot-long beams of soft, opaque, pulsating light.

During the period of pre-Civil War settlement in Arkansas Territory, a healthy wolf population existed throughout the state. Red wolves were the most numerous, but large packs of timber wolves roamed throughout much of the Ozark Mountains. As usually happens in the case of these animals, tales of attacks and predation on livestock were common, although actual proof was seldom forthcoming.

Following the war, human settlement increased and the growing demand for space for cattle and other livestock, as well as for crop farming, disturbed most of the natural environment and displaced much of the wildlife, particularly the predators. Eventually, because of reduced deer populations, the wolves, according to the local farmers, began preying on the most available food in the area—the domestic cattle. In response, the farmers and ranchers ruthlessly hunted, trapped, and poisoned the wolves at every opportunity. By the 1930s, wildlife experts recorded that timber wolves had been virtually exterminated from the state of Arkansas.

Many Arkansans believed that the removal of the timber wolves from the area was a blessing, and that their children and livestock were now safe from this perceived menace. The truth is, there exist no authenticated reports that humans ever suffered from wolf attacks in the state of Arkansas.

It may be true that timber wolves no longer reside in Arkansas, but the elusive spirit of at least one of them continues to prowl the fields, woods, and stream bottoms of southwestern Cleburne County, occasionally frightening and mystifying the residents and causing the local domestic dogs to become agitated and excited.

Skeptics scoff at the notion of a ghost wolf, but evidence suggests that something is happening in these Ozark foothills, something not easily explained. The residents who have seen the wolf are quick to point out that the skeptics are not around when the ghost appears.

Intermittent sightings of the ghost wolf, along with occasional reports of its howling, have been noted since the mid-1940s. The sightings are all similar: The ghost wolf suddenly appears, generally in an open field; sometimes it is seen loping a short distance before stopping, sometimes it remains standing and stationary, and sometimes it is seen just sitting quietly; it vanishes just as quickly and mysteriously as it appears; curious beams of light appear to radiate at least twelve inches from the white body of the wolf.

The ghost wolf has been described as being very large, much bigger than an adult German Shepherd. Though residents who have seen the ghost often express some level of fear and concern, there is no record that the apparition has ever harmed anyone or any livestock.

Sometimes the ghost wolf is heard but not seen, its characteristic howl occasionally echoing across the rolling hills of the region. A wolf howl is distinctly different from that of a coyote or dog, and there is no doubt that it was the call of a timber wolf that sent chills up the spines of area residents over the years.

On the night of April 26, 1995, the howling of a wolf awakened several rural families living a few miles east of Quitman. Three weeks later during a full moon, the ghost wolf appeared in the same area several times and was spotted by no less than six people. Each time the wolf was seen, it was sitting or standing in a field about seventy-five yards from the road and emanating an other worldly glow.

The following morning when investigators examined the region for tracks, nothing could be found even though the dirt in the field bore prints of other animals.

Though the ghost wolf is often seen in fields where cattle graze, no livestock has ever been harmed. Even though the image may be only a few feet away from them, cattle don't seem to notice it at all. On the other hand, domestic dogs become very nervous and almost uncontrollable when the ghost wolf is seen or heard.

The origin of the ghost wolf is shrouded in mystery. Though apparently not threatening, the Cleburne County wolf continues to perplex and frighten those who know for certain it is there.

Oklahoma's Satan Wolf

Cleburne County, Arkansas, is not the only place in the Ozarks from which reports of ghost wolves have emanated. In the Oklahoma Ozarks not far from the present-day town of Disney, a black wolf believed by many of the area residents to be an incarnation of Satan has terrorized residents for many years before finally being appeased by what many believe was the soul of an old Indian.

The first time anyone ever heard of Delaware County's ghost wolf was during the 1880s. Over the course of several weeks, packs of wolves were believed to be responsible for the killing of dozens of head of cattle in the region. Sometimes only a single cow would be killed. Other times groups of three or four would be found slain and partially eaten. Area ranchers rode throughout the countryside hunting, trapping, and poisoning as many wolves as they could, but the predation continued.

After several more weeks passed, it became clear to the ranchers that the killings were being done by a single wolf—a large, black animal that was only seen at night, and whose eyes shone like tiny balls of flame in the moonlight.

The wolf was never seen during the day, always managed to elude the hunters, and consistently avoided traps that were set throughout the area known to be frequented by the animal. On several occasions, it was obvious the wolf had taken the bait out of a trap without springing it.

One evening two brothers—Jake and James Coffield—heard a wolf howl just beyond the field where they pastured a herd of some thirty cattle. Fearing an attack on their livestock, the brothers each armed themselves with a rifle, mounted their horses, and rode out in search of the wolf, determined they would be the ones to finally find and kill the animal and put an end to the predations once and for all.

As they rode down the tree-lined path that paralleled one side of their field, they listened intently for the wolf, but all was silence save for the clopping of the horses' hooves on the dirt trail. The air was very still and there was no movement whatsoever from the trees and brush that grew close to the edge of the road. Light from a waxing moon filtered through the trees providing a small amount of illumination, barely allowing the brothers to view the road a short distance ahead of them.

Suddenly, just as the two riders rounded a bend, they spotted a huge black wolf about forty yards ahead of them standing in the road, facing them. The brothers reined up and regarded the wolf which stood unmoving, its eyes reflecting the light from the moon. A low growl could be heard coming from deep within the animal's throat.

After pausing for a moment, Jake and James each checked their rifles to make certain they were loaded and ready to fire. Without saying a word, they nudged their horses forward at a slow walk.

Closer and closer they came to the wolf until they were within only ten yards of it. The animal still had not moved except to watch the riders intently with its piercing, glowing eyes.

Slowly, James Coffield raised his rifle to his shoulder, took aim, and fired a bullet directly into the head of the wolf. Both horses jumped and bucked at the shot, but after a few seconds they were quickly calmed by their riders. When Jake and James looked again toward the wolf, it was still standing precisely where it had been before the shot, apparently unharmed. James was certain he could not have possibly missed the target with a rifle at such a close range.

This time, Jake nudged his horse forward a few paces and fired his rifle almost point blank into the wolf's head, again with no effect. Three more times, each of the men shot at the wolf, and each time the bullets seemed to pass right through the animal, having no effect whatsoever. Presently, the wolf cocked its head slightly at the brothers, then turned and calmly strode away down the middle of the narrow trail.

Jake and James Coffield looked at each other in astonishment, reloaded their weapons, and charged off in pursuit of the wolf. Rounding another bend in the trail, they pulled up and looked in all directions. It was gone.

The two brothers searched for the animal until dawn, hoping they would find it dead or seriously wounded, but could locate no trace of it. When it was light enough to see, the two men were returning along the tree-lined path they had ridden earlier and noticed that the wolf had left no tracks in the dirt.

When the story of the failed attempt at killing the black wolf was told and retold around the region, the residents grew convinced that this was no ordinary animal they were dealing with—they were convinced it was a ghost. Livestock was now guarded more closely, sometimes twenty-four hours a day. Doors and windows were locked at night, and children were warned not to venture too far from their homes.

For months, and in spite of the closely watched livestock, the wolf's depredations on livestock continued unabated. The wily canine eluded hunters and traps, and appeared to move about at will, striking with a fury, and seemingly daring anyone and everyone to pursue him. Time and again he was seen, and at night he could be heard howling in the distance. Somehow the mysterious animal successfully eluded capture and death.

One day an old Indian arrived in the region and established a poor camp in a grove of trees not far from the bank of a small stream. The old man survived on rabbits he snared in the woods and wild vegetables he harvested. Sometimes a friendly farmer would leave him some garden produce.

One afternoon, a party of riders stopped at the Indian's camp and warned him about the wolf in the vicinity. He told the men that the wolf was the reason he had come, and then he related a strange story.

For many generations, he said, this same wolf had plagued his tribe. After the Indians settled in the region, the wolf attacked and killed horses and cattle, and occasionally even a man. Tribal stories relate that no less than two children were carried off by the ghost wolf, never to be seen again. The wolf, he told the riders, was a manifestation of what the white people called Satan. No bullets could kill the wolf, he stated, and there was no poison strong enough to cause it harm. The Satan Wolf, said the Indian, was only amused by traps and the efforts of the hunters to capture or kill it.

There was only one way to rid the countryside of the wolf, said the old man, and that was to give it what it wanted. When asked what that was, he replied—a human soul.

That is why he was here, he told them. In a recent dream, he was instructed by the spirits of his forefathers to journey to this place and offer himself to the wolf. Once he was accepted by the animal, his ancestors could rest in peace and the wolf would leave the valley and no longer threaten livestock or man.

The riders did not believe the Indian's story, but patiently listened to him, remained courteous, gave him a pouch of tobacco, and finally rode away.

One week later, the same group of riders happened to pass by the old Indian's camp. They hailed him but received no response. Dismounting, they tied their horses to a bush and walked into the camp.

The coals from the campfire were several days old, and the old battered cooking pot was tipped over. The old Indian's lean-to was torn down, as if by a wild animal.

Suddenly, one of the men called out and pointed to something on the ground. It was blood. In fact, as they looked around the abandoned campsite, blood was everywhere. Here and there, they also found pieces of torn clothing that was identical to what the old Indian had been wearing the last time he was seen. For the next hour, the riders searched throughout the immediate area but found no sign of the Indian, dead or alive.

And that night, for the first time in many months, the wolf was not heard. The following morning, and for many mornings thereafter, not a single rancher reported an attack on his livestock.

With cautious optimism, the residents of the vast farming region that paralleled the river listened each night for the Satan Wolf, as it was now being called, but they heard nothing.

Years passed with no more depredations, and the story was told that the Satan Wolf was appeased by the sacrifice the old Indian made of his own soul.

Though relieved, the ranchers were not complacent. Throughout the ensuing years, the distant howling of a wolf could sometimes be heard echoing up and down the river valley. Though no cattle were attacked, the residents remained wary.

Even today, someone will occasionally report the howling of a wolf in the area. Some say it's just a coyote, others say it's only dogs. Old-timers, however, are convinced it's the Satan Wolf, and that it's reminding all that it is not far away.

Ghost Horse of Benton County

On a remote and sparsely populated stretch of unpaved road in Jasper County, Missouri, a horse, a dun mare, is sometimes spotted behind an old rusty, sagging barbed wire fence. Observers claim the animal appears to be searching for something or someone, pacing back and forth behind the wire fence as it stares intently down the road. Then, suddenly and with no warning, the horse will disappear, only to reappear several days later near the same spot.

A few of the nearby residents in this southwestern Missouri county will patiently listen to the newcomers' stories of encounters with this horse and then explain to them that the same animal has been seen here many times over the years—since 1925!

Jasper County's population began growing significantly during the late 1860s when immigrants moved in from Tennessee, Kentucky, and Alabama. Here they found good water, fertile soil, abundant timber, and decent graze for livestock.

Initially, there were a few hostile encounters with area Indians, but eventually peace and harmony reigned. Drought occasionally drove some families away, and severe storms and harsh winters often exacted a toll. Though hardships were many, the hardy and more determined residents remained to carve out a living in this somewhat remote yet entirely peaceful setting.

Barns and cabins were constructed, and eventually small towns with schools and churches began to dot the countryside. A spirit of community and cooperation prevailed, an important bond reinforced by the need for survival in this sometimes harsh landscape.

In the mid-1890s, a baby boy was born into a small Ozark hamlet in Jasper County. A descendant of the original settlers, he grew into an intelligent, charming, and hard-working youngster admired by everyone in the community.

The boy's prized possession was a gentle mare given to him by his father. Expertly broken to the saddle, the mare carried the boy on hundreds of rides across the fields and deep into the woods over the years. The boy cared deeply for the animal, groomed it regularly, and saw to its needs constantly. It was clear that a special relationship had developed between the boy and the horse.

In 1917, the boy, now a young man, was about to be married to a girl from a neighboring community. The two spent a great deal of time together, and, other than his mare, she seemed to be the only thing that occupied his thoughts.

Weeks before the two were to be married, the United States became heavily involved in World War I. Realizing an obligation to his country, the young man enlisted into the army and was shipped to France a short time later. The marriage was postponed until such time as he returned from the war.

On November 11, 1918—seventeen month's following the young man's enlistment—Armistice was declared and the soldiers were to be sent home. Celebrations were held in the tiny Ozark community in anticipation of the young man's return, and wedding plans were resumed.

A few days following the Armistice, the mare began to act strangely. While the town reveled in the good news of the war's end, the horse was often seen pacing nervously in the pasture, stopping now and then to look down the road as if expecting someone.

The family related that, two days following the Armistice, the mare broke through the pasture fence and, when the family awoke the next morning, was found standing outside her master's bedroom window.

The gentle, easy-going mare had never behaved this way in the past, and the family attributed it to advanced age. That afternoon, the fence was repaired and the mare was led back to the pasture.

The next evening, however, the mare broke out again and returned to the same place just outside the window. This time, she knocked the screen out and pushed her head into the room. When the young man's mother entered the room, she saw the horse frantically casting about as if searching the interior for someone. At that point, the family began to suspect that something terrible had happened to the son.

Two days later, the family received a telegram that the young man had been killed in one of the final battles of the war, just hours before the Armistice.

The mare lived on for another seven years and finally died quietly in the pasture. She was buried in a corner of the field under a large oak tree.

Several months following the death of the mare, a passer-by reported seeing it standing against the fence near the road. When he told the young man's family, they assumed he was just mistaken. As weeks passed, however, others reported seeing the mare positioned near the road, staring in the distance as if in anticipation of someone's arrival.

As towns like Joplin and Carthage grew up in this region and employment opportunities increased, more and more people left the small family farms and moved into the city. Many of the tiny communities and farms were simply abandoned and left to ruin.

Today, people often drive along the scenic roads that linked some of these early settlements. Tourists and natives alike revel in the autumn foliage of the countryside, stopping now and then to inspect an old log barn or abandoned homeplace to take photographs of these reminders of times past.

And once in a while, someone will comment on spotting a strange mare while passing by a remote, long-unused pasture. The mare, oblivious to the travelers, looks fixedly down the lonely road as if expecting someone special to arrive.

The traveler may glance away for a second, and when he looks back, the mare is gone.

Monsters

The Devil in Pope County

Big Piney Creek, a favorite canoeing stream with many Arkansawyers as well as a number of out-of-staters aware of its numerous challenges, flows through Arkansas' Johnson and Pope Counties until it finally enters the Arkansas River at Lake Darndanelle. Very few people live in the valley of the Big Piney Creek, and a few long-time residents in nearby Dover say it's because the devil resides there. Beyond that, very few of them care to talk about it.

Since the earliest settlers arrived in this somewhat isolated western part of Pope County, reports of something strange and evil living in the Big Piney bottoms have filtered out of the area and into local lore and legend. Even the Indians who once lived throughout much of this part of Arkansas generally avoided the area of the Big Piney, claiming that truly horrible demons lurked in these dense woods. The first white settlers in the region reported encountering strange forms in the bottoms, creatures never before seen. A number of those who first attempted to homestead the surrounding area were so frightened by what they saw and heard that they soon packed up and moved away. Even today, the region of the Big Piney bottoms is sparsely settled.

According to the late Piney Page, a lifetime Pope County resident who collected hundreds of stories and bits and pieces of fact and folklore from the region, the devil was seen by several people living near Moccasin Creek around 1980.

One story tells of a strange encounter during a deer hunting trip to the Big Piney bottoms. Four men drove to the area from Little Rock, arriving just after dawn. After parking their vehicle, checking their rifles and gear, and donning jackets to warm them against the chilly autumn air, they set off hiking along a narrow game trail not far from the creek. After they were on the trail for about ten minutes, they were suddenly startled by a large, terrifying form that flew out of the trees and landed in the trail about twenty feet in front of them.

The deer hunters described the bizarre figure as dark, with greenish-black skin like a snake, and it sported a pair of huge, black wings. The creature stood upright like a man on legs that appeared thin and spindly. The face was reptilian, and one of the hunters later claimed he saw a forked tongue flicking out of the thin, cruel-looking mouth.

Pausing only a for moment to assess the hunters, the creature suddenly advanced toward them, lurching forward a few steps and emitting a piercing scream. Frightened beyond words, the men threw down their rifles, turned, and fled from the area, never to return.

On the way back to Little Rock, the four men agreed among themselves not to tell a soul of what they had seen. They were afraid no one would believe them, that they would be laughed at and derided. Years later, when one of them finally relented and related the terrifying experience, he learned that, over the years, several residents of the Big Piney area had seen the same beast.

* * *

During the 1950s, parties of canoeists, testing the sometimes tricky yet popular waters of Big Piney Creek, often returned home with stories of encounters with an unknown creature, stories so bizarre that no one would believe them. One group of terrified boaters reported to the county sheriff that they saw a man-like form with huge, black wings flying back and forth across the stream as they paddled near a location known as Long Pool. The creature, evidently enraged by the intrusion, screamed and hissed at the canoeists. According to one member of the group, the monster had yellow eyes that burned like fire in a head that looked like it belonged to a lizard. All of the boaters remarked on the powerful and repulsive stench they detected following its appearance.

Another tale involving this strange and fearsome creature allegedly occurred in 1965. Late one evening, the twelve-year-old daughter of a local farmer was sent to pick up an afternoon newspaper at the home of an uncle. To get to the uncle's house, the girl had to walk along a narrow path through the dark woods. The uncle, who lived about one-quarter mile away, saved the paper every day for his brother who sent one of his four children to fetch it each evening around six o'clock. It was considered a small honor to be the one to retrieve the paper from the favorite uncle, and the children often competed for the opportunity to do so.

It was well past six one evening, but no one had arrived at the uncle's house to pick up the newspaper. The uncle grew concerned. It was late November and very cold, so he decided to go out and see if one of his nephew's children was coming up the path. After buttoning up his heavy coat, placing his hat on his head, and throwing another white oak split on the fire, he left his house and made his way down the trail linking his home with that of his brother.

After he had been on the trail about five minutes, the uncle heard a child weeping, and on investigating he found his niece cowering next to the bole of a large tree. As he approached her, the girl began screaming and crying out that the devil was after her. After finally calming her down, the uncle carried the girl back to his house, placed her near the warm fire, and listened intently as she related her strange and terrifying experience, stopping now and then in an attempt to get her to pull herself together and control her sobbing.

As the little girl was walking down the road, she explained, she heard strange noises coming from the dense woods to her left. Whatever was making the sounds was following her, and she was worried it might be a cougar or a bear. A cougar had been spotted several days earlier in the area, and residents were concerned. Growing scared, the girl said, she broke into a run. At the same time, the sounds in the woods grew louder. Suddenly, several yards away in the trail ahead, a crouching figure burst out of the forest and stopped, confronting her.

Stretching to its full height, the thing in the trail spread a great set of dark wings. It was a creature she had never seen before, but had heard about many times. All around her the cold November air seemed to turn warm and the early evening sky appeared to darken perceptibly. The frightened little girl was convinced that standing before her was the devil himself.

Spitting and hissing, the creature stalked toward the child on long, thin legs, sometimes taking long strides, sometimes hopping like a bird! When it finally stood directly in front of her, it bent low and positioned its reptilian face directly in front of hers.

The devil, according to the little girl, smelled like burnt, rotten meat, and she thought she would faint from the thick and heavy stench.

Yellow eyes burned into hers as she retreated backward. From time to time, a long forked tongue shot out from the wicked mouth of the beast, coming within scant inches of her face.

Without warning, the creature emitted a high, piercing shriek and, flapping its mighty wings, shot upward and flew away over the treetops. It was the last thing the girl saw before she collapsed in a faint and was found several minutes later by her uncle.

The young girl who experienced that terrifying night is now a grown woman living in Russellville, Arkansas. More than thirty years after the incident, she still breaks down in sobs and trembles each time she recalls it. To this day, she is firmly convinced she was visited by Satan himself.

A late evening visit to the Big Piney bottoms almost any time of the year yields a number of strange sensations. While the gurgling flow of the stream provides a steady rhythm of background sound, the darkness of the nearby woods contributes an eerie, prickly feel along with a number of curious, undefinable noises.

Now and again, people who visit these woods try to describe the sounds they hear coming from just beyond their vision, sounds emanating from a variety of locations. Visitors report hearing distant and muffled hissing, and even screaming. Heavy footfalls in the forest are sometimes heard. Other times, a sound described as the flapping of heavy, leathery wings is perceived. Most of the time, the sounds come from the dense, low-growing brush in the forest. Other times, they seem to come from high in the trees.

Everyone who has heard the sounds agrees that something evil lives here.

The White River Monster

Along the eastern edge of the Ozark Mountains and somewhere along a stretch of the muddy waters of the White River near the Jackson County town of Newport, Arkansas, lurks a strange and unknown creature that defies explanation. For hundreds of years, the Indians who originally occupied this area were aware of the existence of this mysterious beast. These days, this curious denizen of the river is called the White River Monster—it has been observed by hundreds of people over the years, yet remains elusive and mysterious.

During an early visit to the White River region during the 1700s by the noted French explorer Father Jacques Marquette, the priest wrote in his journal about an encounter he had with "monstrous fish which struck so violently against our canoes that we took them to be large trees." Marquette, though clearly terrified by his experience, provided very little description of the creature.

During the early 1850s when westward-migrating settlers began moving into the White River region of northeastern Arkansas to take advantage of the fertile soils found there, they were greeted and welcomed by the Quapaw Indians, a friendly, peaceful tribe that had farmed the land in the area for ages. In addition to sharing the bounty of the earth with their white neighbors, the Indians also taught them many of their customs and related a number of their folktales.

One oft-told Quapaw tale was that of a strange monster that lived in the murky waters of the nearby White River. According to the Indians, the monster had been observed over many years by several generations of the tribe. It was so large, it was said, that it was often mistaken for an island as it floated on the surface of the stream. The monster would remain in the area for several days and then disappear. Sometimes, many years would pass before it reappeared, but over time an odd pattern of occurrences became apparent—the White River creature showed approximately every thirty years.

More concerned with the agricultural potential of the fertile soils of the White River's floodplain and the establishment of a stable community with schools and churches, the newcomers busied themselves with the planting and harvesting of crops and planning for the future. They paid scant attention to bizarre stories of a river monster. For the most part, the settlers passed the tales off as wild and unbelievable Indian stories with no basis in truth whatsoever.

Over time the numbers of settlers increased, and as they planted and harvested bounties of corn, cotton, wheat, beans, and other crops over the next few years, their successes attracted even more migrants who arrived by wagon and on foot from the east and also settled in the region.

Before long, towns such as Newport, Batesville, and Augusta sprang up along the shores of the White River and into the foothills of the Ozark Mountains. Eventually, these newcomers were also treated to the stories of the White River Monster by their Indian neighbors.

One curious Indian tale relates that a young Quapaw Indian spotted the creature out in the middle of the river one day and decided to row his canoe over to it. On approaching the large form in the water, the Indian noted that its skin was milky white, bare, and very slippery. Curious, the brave poked the end of his wooden paddle into the flesh. Each stroke left a small impression in the skin. Finally, after deciding the curious beast was harmless, he climbed onto the exposed surface and walked around on top of it.

Apparently awakened by the presence of the Indian on its back, the creature responded suddenly to the intrusion by thrashing around. The monster succeeded in hurling the Indian into the river, and as the frightened Quapaw swam furiously toward the nearby shore, the creature gradually ceased its pitching and moved slowly downstream.

On hearing these tales, the settlers generally laughed and scoffed, and claimed that such a creature could not possibly exist. Amused, they continued about their business of farming and building communities. A short time later, however, the strange denizen of the White River that had made such a great impression on the Indians made another appearance and convinced hundreds of people that something bizarre and unexplainable lived in the waters of the White River.

When the War Between the States was well under way, a Confederate paddleboat carrying just over one million dollars in gold coins steamed slowly upstream on the White River. Bound for Batesville, the gold was to be delivered to a military encampment where it was intended as payment for Rebel troops in the field. All along the river route, the officers and crew of the boat kept a wary eye out for Union raiders.

Moments after passing Newport, the Rebel craft was jerked violently as a result of a sudden blow to the bow. Believing the vessel was under attack from Yankees, the captain ran forward to assess the damage. As he arrived at the bow, there was a second sharp impact which knocked him to the deck. Crawling to the rail, the captain pulled himself up and spotted a huge hole in the hull planking.

As the boat took on water and began sinking, the captain, along with a dozen troopers, was suddenly surprised by the appearance of a huge creature a short distance upstream. The large, unknown animal was rolling and tossing about in the water as if upset or angry, generating high waves which rocked the injured vessel. Stunned into temporary immobility, the soldiers could only watch as the angry and terrifying monster leaped and splashed in the stream just yards away.

Moments later, the boat sank to the bottom of the river, carrying with it small fortune in gold and two dozen Confederate soldiers.

In 1890, the White River Monster, as it was now being called, appeared once again, remained in the Newport area for several days, and was observed by dozens of area residents. Forty-seven years passed before the monster was seen again.

In July, 1937, several prominent Newport citizens reported observing a huge creature creating a great disturbance out in the middle of the White River. Rolling, leaping, and plunging in the stream, the monster created huge waves which crashed onto the shore as far as one hundred yards away.

For nearly a year, the White River Monster remained in the area, and was seen by residents many times as it moved up and down the stream near Newport. During this time, the creature was described by many as "huge," "as large as a whale," and "cream-colored."

Newport resident Bramlett Bateman lived in a house on the bank of the White River in 1937. For hours at a time, he claimed, he would watch the monster swimming and "frolicking" in the river. Bateman claimed he had observed the creature on at least one hundred different occasions for over a year, and he described it as being about twelve feet long and four to five feet wide. According to Bateman, the monster never showed a head or a tail.

So common were the appearances of the White River Monster near Bateman's house that he began charging a fee to the hordes of people who wanted to view it from his vantage point.

As suddenly as it appeared, the White River Monster vanished during autumn of 1938 and was not seen again for twenty-eight years.

In 1966, Vernon Tucker, Dorothy Day, and Mary Jo Skinner encountered a strange creature while fishing. Shortly after the sun went down, the three friends began setting out trotlines in the hope of catching a number of catfish. Tucker, pointing his flashlight over the prow of the craft, guided the way as the boat moved slowly through the water, the outboard motor idling quietly. Suddenly something up ahead of the boat captured Tucker's attention. He said later it sounded like someone had fallen in the water. Manning the throttle, he sped toward the sound.

Nearing the point where he thought he heard the noise, something huge rose up out of the water, something unlike any of the three had ever seen before. Skinner claimed the creature was gray and appeared to be sparsely covered with hair. The creature looked straight at the boat and Skinner recalled that the head and face was similar to that of a huge monkey. The creature remained motionless for a few seconds as it regarded the trio, then it suddenly flipped over and swam away. The tail, said Skinner, reminded her of those normally associated with mermaids. Tucker said the creature had flippers and swam very fast.

In June, 1971, a well-known and respected Newport resident was walking along the bank of the river early one morning when he spotted a creature about "the size of a boxcar" swimming and rolling out near the center of the stream and causing waves approximately three feet high. The man watched the monster for almost fifteen minutes from about one hundred and fifty feet away, and reported that it had "a smooth skin that appeared to be peeling."

Two days later, another Newport resident named Ernest Denks admitted he had seen the monster a week earlier, but was afraid to say anything for fear no one would believe him and that he would be ridiculed. When he finally agreed to be interviewed years later, Denks decided to tell about his experience. He estimated the creature weighed one thousand pounds, and described it very long, grey in color and had a "long, pointed bone protruding from its forehead." He also stated "it looked like it came from the ocean" and described it as "the darndest looking animal I have ever seen."

Denks called the creature "The Eater," because, as he said, "it looked like it could eat anything, anywhere, anytime."

Several days following Denks' revelation, on 29 June, three fishermen reported an encounter with the monster. They claimed it was about two hundred feet from their boat when it suddenly began to roll about in the water, creating huge waves. One of the men, Cloyce Warren, said it was a "giant form that rose to the surface and began moving in the middle of the river." He described it as "long and gray-colored" and looked like something "prehistoric." Warren took a Polaroid photograph of the creature. After the film was processed, however, the image appeared mostly as a blur, showing only a grey form amidst a swirl of foam and ripples. The image in the photo looked as if it possessed a spiny backbone, approximately thirty feet of which was exposed above the surface of the water.

Other Newport citizens, heretofore silent about their experiences, now began coming forth with reports of sightings. In all, about one hundred and fifty people claimed to have seen the monster. Most of the witnesses declared it to be about thirty feet long, and a few stated it had fins.

Several days later, yet another Newport resident named Lloyd Hamilton, took a photograph of what he described as a "spiny-backed monster." Unfortunately,

Hamilton's color film was accidentally processed as black and white and revealed nothing.

In July 1971, Ollie Richardson and Joey Dupree set out in a boat to go fishing on the White River near Bateman Bend. Richardson, sixty-six years old at the time, was steering the boat upstream on a course near the shore when something struck the underside of the craft. The impact was so great it lifted the boat completely out of the water. Whatever it was never surfaced. Richardson described it later that day as "something very large and alive."

Three weeks later, two men fishing on the White River reported a strange experience to Jackson County Sheriff Ralph Henderson. After landing their boat on Towhead Island, they said, they encountered the tracks of some huge, unidentifiable creature in the sand.

Sheriff Henderson, in the company of several other law enforcement officers and a game warden, went to Towhead Island to examine the tracks for themselves. Game warden Claude Foshee was startled at the size of the prints and admitted he had never seen anything like them before. The tracks were almost fourteen inches long, eight inches across, and each included the imprint of three clawed toes, a large heel pad, and a spur extending from the rear of the foot. Warden Foshee measured an impressive distance of eight feet between each track.

As Sheriff Henderson made plaster casts of the tracks, Warden Foshee explored around the island for other signs of the beast. He eventually came to a location near the shore where the grass had been mashed flat as if something extremely large and heavy had laid on it.

* * *

Since 1971, there have been no authenticated sightings of the White River Monster. Skeptics claim there is no monster at all, and that people were only seeing large fish, probably alligator gars or catfish. Alligator gar, in fact, were once quite common in the White River, and the state record gar for Arkansas is eight feet, three inches long, with a weight of 350 pounds.

The late Jimmy Driftwood, a Grammy Award-winning songwriter and folk performer who lived near the White River, said years ago some who professed to be "authorities" offered the opinion that the creature was a manatee, a rare species of underwater mammal found these days in Florida. Decades ago when manatees were more common, according to Driftwood, they would sometimes be spotted swimming in the White River near Newport.

Manatees, however, are rather docile creatures, are not nearly as big as boxcars, do not have spiny backbones, do not possess a long, pointed bone protruding from their foreheads, and don't thrash around in the water as the monster has been alleged to do.

Others have suggested the creature might be an alligator, some have offered the opinion it was a porpoise, and a few even insisted it was a shark.

Though some may find reason to doubt the existence of the White River Monster, the truth is that, whatever it is, it has shown itself not only to the native Indians who lived along the river, but also to the earliest white settlers who migrated here from the east, as well as to a number of the current residents of Newport. The monster has appeared approximately every thirty years or so for the past two hundred years or more.

The White River Monster has never been adequately explained by believers or skeptics. Whitey, as the monster has been called in recent years, continues to baffle the experts.

The Water Panther

Long before the first Spanish and French explorers ever arrived in the Ozark Mountains, the Indians who lived, farmed, hunted, and trapped along the fertile bottomlands of the Little Red River near the present-day town of Heber Springs in Cleburne County often spoke of a strange and frightening creature commonly seen in the woods and the water. This creature was known to terrorize their villages, attack and kill horses, and prey on members of the tribe.

This creature, which the Indians called a water panther, was believed by them to be a spirit-monster, and according to legend it, or its descendants, has lived here for ages in a limestone cave. The water panther, according to the Indians, was part human and walked upright. It was described as having a slight hump between the shoulders, a head and neck that jutted forward, and was covered in thick, black fur much like a bear. The face of the creature has been described by some as cat-like, by others as reptilian, by a few as fish-like. There are one or two references that refer to bear-like features. In every case, however, the creature went about on two feet much like a human being and was reputed to move through the woods and bottomlands with surprising speed. The Indians regarded it unlucky to look upon the water panther, and those that did were considered to be cursed by other members of the tribe.

It was also believed by the Indians that the water panther preyed on human beings in order to survive.

Early trappers who entered the region of the Little Red River often spoke of encountering the water panther and of hearing its frightening cries at night, cries that were described as being a cross between the "cry of a panther and the scream of Satan himself." The trappers tried to hunt the elusive creature, but claimed their bullets could not penetrate its hide. Traps that were set for it were often found sprung, but whatever was caught had sufficient strength and dexterity to open them and escape. Several mysterious deaths were attributed by the trappers to the water panther. The victims were often found torn limb from limb.

When loggers moved into this area during the 1870s and 1880s, they, too, reported the presence of a monster which, they claimed, sometimes stalked them in the woods. As before, there were reports of killings that were attributed to this curious beast, and, in the most recent cases, the unfortunate victims were partially eaten.

Years later as more people moved into the region, many of them hunted deer, raccoons, and rabbits to supplement their food supply. As increasing numbers of hunters entered the woods in search of game, a few of them encountered the water panther. As with the trappers and loggers, a number of strange deaths were blamed on the creature. At night, unearthly screams could be heard from the bottomlands near the river.

After the huge dam which formed Greer's Ferry Lake was completed in the early 1960s and the waters of the Little Red River and other tributaries were backed up, the bottomlands most frequented by the water panther were now inundated. Sightings of the enigmatic monster gradually decreased, and then ceased altogether. At least for a while.

Beginning around 1966, sightings of the water panther were reported with frightening regularity. Rather than roaming and stalking the wooded bottoms of the Little Red River as before, the creature was sometimes spotted swimming in the lake that now covered the ancient homeland of the Indians. On different occasions, at least three people claimed they saw the water panther entering or leaving a cave located on the northern shore of the lake, a partially submerged natural opening in a sheer limestone cliff.

For a number of years, though never proven, several mysterious drownings in Greer's Ferry Lake were attributed to the water panther. The bodies were never found, and several nearby residents expressed the belief that the victims were eaten by the creature.

In the early 1970s, a SCUBA diver reported an encounter with the monster near an underwater opening to a cavern. The creature, which he described as a horrid, man-like form covered with thick, dense fur, rushed at the diver from the cavern and ripped off his mask. Frightened for his life, the diver kicked and flailed and succeeded in fending off the beast until he could reach the surface and safety. He was subsequently treated for severe lacerations and shock. Later, the diver claimed the creature moved with astonishing speed through the water but had no visible fins or flippers.

Years ago, former Arkansas Senator John McClelland had a splendid home constructed on a bluff overlooking Greer's Ferry Lake. Just below the house, a natural cave opened out onto the water below, and McClelland decided it would serve nicely as a boat house. To facilitate passage from his house to his boat, McClelland had an elevator installed in a sinkhole that connected the cave with the slope near his home. The crew that was hired to install the elevator worked in terror, for during the entire time they labored they were, in their words, "subjected to the hellish screams and agonizing cries of some hideous creature living in the hole."

Many dismiss the tales of the water panther as mere fanciful folklore, designed only to scare the wits out of the gullible. Others, however, many of them long-time residents of the area, are not so sure.

Sometimes at night, they claim, they can still hear the eerie cries of the water panther echoing across the lake.

The Lake Conway Monster

During the early 1950s, Arkansas' Lake Conway, located in Faulkner County, was gaining a regional reputation as an excellent place to fish for bream, bass, catfish, and near record-size crappie. Reports of successful fishing and published photographs showing fishermen with large strings of fish attracted sportsmen from all over the state, and in time the lake began to draw visitors from much of the rest of the country. Today, Lake Conway remains one of the most popular fishing locations in the state of Arkansas.

Despite the growing appeal of Lake Conway to sportsmen during the past few decades, shoreline residents quietly maintained there was something in the lake, something strange, terrifying, and unexplainable. They claimed a mysterious creature resided in the water and along the shore, a frightening form that was active only at night. The creature, though it never harmed anyone, was known to attack fishermen in their boats.

On several occasions, startled anglers fled from the lake, insisting that something huge made sharp and sudden contact with their boats, nearly capsizing them. Skeptics suggested it may have only been a large snapping turtle, perhaps even an alligator, but during the successive months as the strange encounters continued, the fishermen began reporting seeing something in the water. What they saw was clearly not a large snapping turtle or an alligator, but a strange object, a shape that was like nothing they had ever seen before.

A few of the Lake Conway regulars claimed that what they saw was a man-like creature with terrifying features wading in the shallow waters after sundown. Most, however, initially refrained from talking about it for fear they would be ridiculed. Only after a passage of many years did some of the fishermen come forth with stories of encounters with what has come to be called the Lake Conway Monster

Long before Lake Conway was formed, farmers and others who lived near the towns of Mayflower and Saltillo often commented about a strange creature sometimes seen prowling in the creek bottoms. The "thing," as they called it, was seldom observed up close, and early descriptions of it referred only to a shadowy form with a humped back. On noting that it was observed, the creature bounded away, employing a curious kind of locomotion some have referred to as hopping, much like a kangaroo. Sometimes the thing was seen splashing through the creeks seemingly searching for food, and other times it was spotted crashing through the bottoms as if it were pursuing something, perhaps a small mammal destined to become a meal. Finally, one man saw the monster up close. Too close.

One night in 1952, George Dillon, a Mayflower resident, had rowed about one hundreds yards from the Lake Conway shore, intent on checking his trotlines. One of the lines was snagged in about six feet of water, and after fighting it for several minutes, Dillon managed to pull it free. Feeling a heavy tug on the line, he was certain he had hooked a large catfish.

As Dillon pulled in the line, a form completely alien to him rose to the surface at the end of it. At first, Dillon thought he had hooked the body of a drowning victim, but as the object was pulled closer to the boat, it suddenly rose up and Dillon froze in terror as he gazed into the horrifying face of what he later described as a monster.

Dillon claimed the creature was about the size of a man but had very broad, muscular shoulders, a concave chest, and a large hump on its back. The face, which the fisherman said was grotesque, was long and narrow and resembled that of a monkey. Green, spotted, frog-like skin covered the creature. The wide-open mouth—large and toothless and rimmed with thick blue lips—was bleeding heavily where it had been snagged by the catfish hook. The blood that ran down the chin and neck of the creature, according to Dillon, was black.

As Dillon sat in stunned silence in his boat, the monster placed a large, webbed and clawed hand on the gunwale. At first, Dillon thought the thing was going to try to climb into the craft, but instead it pushed the boat away so suddenly and powerfully that the fisherman was nearly thrown out of it. Grabbing his paddle and forgetting his trotline, Dillon rowed furiously toward shore. On reaching the bank, he turned to look for the creature and saw it swimming slowly away. Eventually it submerged and did not reappear.

Following George Dillon's encounter with the creature, sightings of the Lake Conway Monster occurred regularly for the next three years. During the autumn of 1955, the sightings grew less frequent, and eventually they stopped altogether. Then, for the next twenty years the creature was not seen. Just as lakeshore residents were beginning to believe they were rid of the strange creature, it suddenly reappeared.

A new generation of fishermen was now reporting encounters with the Lake Conway Monster. More often than not, the creature was spotted walking and hopping upright in the shallow water near the shore. As before, it was generally described as being about the size of a man and having a monkey-like face and skin like a frog. One fisherman claimed the monster rose up out of the dark waters one night in front of his boat and hissed at him. Reports of monster sightings continued for several months in 1975 and then suddenly stopped.

Once again, for another twenty years nothing was heard of the Lake Conway Monster, and aside from a few stories repeated by some area old-timers, it was largely forgotten. In 1995, however, following a two-decade absence, the monster returned.

On a quiet and exceptionally warm night in March, 1995, a fisherman—a well known and influential citizen of the nearby town of Conway—was checking his trotlines on the lake when he reached a place where one of them wouldn't yield to his pull. Though he tugged and jerked on the line for several minutes, it would not come up.

The fisherman believed the line was hopelessly snagged on one of the many submerged logs in the lake, and he reached into his tackle box for a utility knife to sever it. As he started to cut the line, it suddenly grew taut in his hand and began pulling away, dragging the boat along behind.

For forty yards, the boat was pulled rapidly toward the middle of the lake when the line abruptly grew slack. For several minutes all was quiet, and the fisherman sat silently in the boat, afraid to make a sound, afraid of what might be in the water just out of sight below the boat. A few seconds later, something beneath him thudded solidly against the underside of the craft, nearly capsizing it. Frightened, the fisherman grabbed onto the gunwales and held tightly.

Just as the ripples from the previous turbulence died down, another sharp and sudden impact was felt and the boat was lifted almost entirely out of the water. Seconds later, something eerie surfaced from the murky lake about three feet from the craft. The fisherman later recalled gazing upon the head and shoulders of "a monster, the most frightening thing I have ever seen or could ever imagine, a face and head straight from the depths of hell."

After regarding the frightened fisherman for several seconds, the monster slowly submerged. Desperately holding back the panic that was surging through his being, the fisherman sat quietly in the boat for several minutes until he was certain the danger had passed, and then paddled back to shore.

Descriptions of the Lake Conway Monster render it unique among the world's mysteries. Some have suggested the creature might be a genetic mutation. A few have offered the notion that it might be some kind of prehistoric creature. Others insist it is likely only a catfish or some other form of wildlife, and that the overactive imaginations of some fishermen have embellished their experiences. One fisherman, who claims to have seen the monster several times, stated, "None of the skeptics have ever fished on Lake Conway at night."

Several anglers who have had encounters with the creature started out as skeptics. One of them, a former university biology professor who initially scoffed at the tales, has subsequently seen the monster on two different occasions.

"There is certainly something strange out there in that lake," he stated, "and whatever it is, it's completely unknown to science."

The Lake Conway Monster remains a mystery, one that continues to baffle the experts and occasionally frighten shoreline residents and visiting fishermen.

The Little People

Monsters come in a variety of sizes.

To most people, monsters are generally perceived as somewhat large, hulking, and normally threatening creatures. Not all monsters are large, however, and some of the most terrifying tales of attack and depredation in the Ozark Mountains are associated with strange creatures reputed to be no more than three feet tall.

The remote regions of the Ozark Mountains where the states of Arkansas, Missouri, and Oklahoma share a common boundary are reputedly the ancient home of a tribe of vicious monsters. What distinguishes these monsters from all others is that they are diminutive, growing to a height of only a few feet. In spite of their relatively small size, however, they have been responsible, according to local folklore and legend, for a number of attacks, for terrorizing Indians and early settlers alike, and for occasionally killing and eating livestock. And humans.

The folklore of several North American Indian tribes contains references to what have generally come to be known as the "little people." For some tribes, these little people are regarded as spirits that inspired and performed positive acts. Some consider them good luck. Other tribes, however, regard the little people as demons with a propensity for evil and for killing.

Early stories of these creatures are attributed to the Osage Indians, early Ozark dwellers who once lived in the aforementioned region. Occasional travelers in the area sometimes mentioned the little people, describing them as consisting of small families or tribes which inhabited the densely wooded portions of the Ozarks here, sometimes living in caves, sometimes in thickets of briars and other undergrowth. Many years before the settlement of white men in this area, the Indians who frequented the region were forced to contend with the depredations of these malicious creatures.

Described as being no more than two-and-a-half to three feet tall, these strange little Ozark people possessed a dark brown skin similar to the color and texture of tanned leather. Covered in a fine, and sometimes sparse, reddish-brown hair that grew about four inches long, they went about totally naked and traveled in bands of six or seven. Furthermore, reports of albino forms of these little people are common.

In addition to their diminutive stature, the most remarkable features of the little people were their fierce visages and their disproportionately long, razor-sharp teeth. Their misshapen heads contained large, cruel, glaring eyes. The movements of these small creatures were quick, almost squirrel-like, and they were capable of running through the woods at a high rate of speed. It was said that a group of them could easily overtake and bring down a mature deer. It has also been said they could move through the trees almost as fast as on the ground.

The little people often attacked the hunting camps of the Indians who frequented the area. One tale relates an incident where a hunting party departed camp, leaving a member to watch over the horses. When the hunters returned the following day, their companion, as well as one of the horses, had been killed and partially eaten by the little people. Before he was slain, the Indian slew one of the tiny monsters, and for years afterward, the curious body was carried from village to village and placed on display. Rumors abound throughout this part of the Ozarks that the mummified remains of the creature came into the possession of one of the early white settlers and was handed down to family members over the generations. Some claim it was eventually placed in a trunk and is currently stored in the attic of a residence somewhere in Delaware County, Oklahoma.

Sometime during the 1950s, a reporter from an Oklahoma City newspaper allegedly tracked down the owners of the little monster and was allowed to view it. He took several photographs but neither they nor an article were ever published.

Numerous references to the little people have also been found in the journals and diaries of early French explorers who entered this area. Time and again, trapping and exploration parties were forced to fight off nightly attacks by these hideous folk who lurked just beyond the light of the campfires waiting for a chance to dash into the camp and secure a victim.

Early white settlers in the region also reported a number of encounters with the little people during the first half of the nineteenth century. After losing livestock, as well as an occasional citizen, to the fierce and carnivorous creatures, armed parties of men entered the woods and hunted them down, often killing as many as three or four in a single night. After several months of these nightly hunts, the depredations slowed and eventually ceased altogether.

Many, however, do not believe that all of the little people were killed off.

To this day, backpackers and hunters who spend the night in the Ozark woods near the Arkansas-Missouri-Oklahoma border sometimes report strange visits by small forms they describe as human-like in appearance with oversize eyes, grotesque heads, and long, sharp teeth.

Most who listen to these reports scoff at them, claiming they are little more than the products of active imaginations, but those who have seen the little people stick hard and fast to their stories.

Old-timers in the region warn us to listen closely to the reports and to consider them seriously. When interviewed, many of them confess a fear that someday the little people will return in force, and no one living in the remote regions of the mountains will be safe.

The Creature with No Face

The following tale is sometimes told in Northwestern Arkansas in the town of Berryville and the neighboring communities. It is related to friends and relatives but seldom to strangers. Many of the residents of that region who know the story of the creature with no face state they are often reluctant to relate the facts to outsiders. For one thing, they are afraid no one will believe them and will think they are making it all up. For another, some of their neighbors are related to those involved in the tale.

During the mid-1960s, travelers along Arkansas State Highway 62 and nearby secondary roads often reported seeing a strange figure darting here and there in the woods and sometimes crossing the roads. Most of the sightings took place at night, and the figure was described as being about the size of a boy. It was always naked but covered in reddish-brown hair. Sometimes the figure would simply dash across the pavement and take cover in the adjacent woods. Other times it would stand in the middle of the road, forcing oncoming vehicles to brake. At least three travelers drove to within ten feet of the being, close enough to provide a detailed description to the county sheriff.

The creature—a term given to the monster by one of the travelers—was about five feet six inches tall and completely naked except for a thin covering of hair. The most startling part of the description, however, had to do with the face. Each of the wayfarers who identified the creature stated that it had no face! One said it had a barely perceptible hole where the mouth should have been; others claimed it had no identifiable facial features whatsoever.

Yet another traveler, a farmer hauling boxed produce in a staked flatbed truck, encountered the creature one warm summer night. Driving slowly down Highway 21 around 10:00 pm, the farmer was suddenly aware of something running in the bar ditch parallel to the road. Looking to his left, the driver was startled to see what he described as a "boy, covered in dark hair, running alongside the truck." Most startling of all, according to the farmer, was the fact that the "boy" appeared to have no face. The "boy" never threatened the driver, and kept pace with him for about one-half mile when it suddenly veered off into the woods. When the farmer reported the incident to the sheriff's department the following day, he referred to the thing he saw as "the wild boy of the Ozarks," and for a time the name stuck.

Throughout the Ozarks just off country roads and lanes are a number of spots favored by high school-age males and females for parking. In 1962, a seventeen-year-old boy and a sixteen-year-old girl, students at Berryville High School, burst into the home of the boy's parents to report a bizarre incident that had happened to them only minutes earlier. It occurred while they were parking, they said, near a ridge located just off state road 221 north of town. The teenagers had been at the spot for about twenty minutes when they heard something scratching on the car near the back window. When they turned to look, they were shocked to see a horrible-looking creature staring back at them through the rear window. The face, if that was what it could be called, seemed to be covered with hair, and the only feature that could be seen was the mouth, a dark, round, gaping hole that dripped saliva. As the two teenagers stared in shocked disbelief at the frightening image, a low moan escaped from the thing. Later, the girl stated that she believed the creature was trying to talk to them, trying to communicate in a desperate kind of way. The boy, his heart pounding heavily with terror, quickly started the engine, shoved the gear into reverse, and backed out of the spot.

At that moment, the faceless monster leaped on top of the vehicle and began scratching on the roof. From time to time it would slap at the side windows as if it were trying to break them. When the driver slammed the shift lever into first gear and stepped on the gas, the creature slid from the roof to the hood of the car and began beating on the front windshield. Negotiating a sharp turn at high speed, the driver managed to dislodge the creature, causing it to slide off the hood and onto the ground. As he sped away, the boy could see it in his rear-view mirror: It was jumping up and down and thrashing about as if very angry.

Nothing was reported of what was now being called the faceless Wild Boy of the Ozarks for several months. Then, in 1970, a group of young boys had been shooting rats at the Berryville city dump when they were, as they said, "attacked" by a monster. Though frightened badly, none of the boys was harmed. The subsequent descriptions of their attacker given to a sheriff's deputy coincided with those of the Wild Boy of the Ozarks.

As the months passed, more and more people reported seeing the creature. All of the descriptions were identical—it appeared to be the size and shape of a boy, it was covered with hair, and it had no face.

Sightings of the Wild Boy continued through 1971. In each case, those who encountered it felt threatened, but no one was ever actually harmed.

One night during the autumn of 1971, a Carroll County deputy sheriff reported an encounter with the Wild Boy. As the deputy was patrolling a dirt road a few miles from town, he was surprised by the sudden appearance of a figure that rose up just ahead of his patrol car, an image illuminated in the glare of the headlights. At first, the deputy thought it was one of the local residents, but as he approached, he saw that the figure was covered with hair, and where the face was supposed to be there was nothing but a slit for a mouth. As the deputy stared at the thing standing before him, he realized he was looking at the oft-reported creature the residents of the area called the Wild Boy of the Ozarks.

This was no boy, the deputy later wrote in his report, for the thing he saw in the glare of his headlights did not appear to be human.

Following the passage of several more months, a curious story emerged. It began with the death of a seventy-year-old woman, a widow, named Hattie and who lived south of Highway 62. After she was found dead in her home, a subsequent investigation determined she died from natural causes. The body was delivered to town where it was prepared for burial.

When sheriff's deputies searched the house and property of the dead woman, they found an old corn crib made from logs out behind the house. Close examination of the crib suggested someone, or something, had been living in it. After questioning some of Hattie's neighbors, a most remarkable story gradually emerged. Approximately thirty years earlier, Hattie had given birth to a boy, a birth that took place in her home and a birth that was never reported. According to her neighbors, there was something terribly wrong with the baby—it was not normal, they said. Away from the mother and among themselves, they referred to the child as a monster. The baby was like any other newborn in every way save for the fact that is was covered with long, fine reddish-brown hair and it had no face.

Knowing that her baby would never be treated properly by schools and authorities, Hattie kept him at home, never letting him out where he could be seen by anyone.

When Hattie's child reached the age of twelve, he would leave the house from time to time and roam throughout the woods and countryside. His hair-covered body and disfigured face frightened neighbors, and occasionally Hattie would be forced to chain the boy in the corn crib. In time, Hattie stopped chaining him, and it is believed he began leaving the premises on a regular basis to wander throughout the area. Though the child apparently had no overt intentions of ever scaring anyone, his bizarre appearance and manner made the neighbors quite nervous, even terrified.

Some claim Hattie's boy only wanted to make contact with fellow humans, that he was lonely and that he longed for companionship. Others maintain the grotesque offspring was dangerous and that he had killed chickens and hogs, ripping their heads from their bodies and drinking the blood.

The truth may never be known. After Hattie's death, the Wild Boy was never seen again. What became of him can only be speculated: Perhaps he still roams the deep and remote Ozark woodlands and bottoms, living off wild game and vegetables; perhaps he wandered to some other remote location where, knowing he would be shunned by normal people, he could live in solitude. Some think he might have died.

Whatever became of the creature with no face has continued to mystify the people living in northwestern Arkansas.

The Buffalo River Monster

Hemmed-In Hollow is an attractive Ozark Mountain site located along the upper reaches of Arkansas' Buffalo River in Newton County. This location has long been a popular place for hiking, picnicking, and related outdoor activities. With each passing year, more and more visitors enjoy the beauty of this part of the Ozarks.

Before white men came to dominate this region, Hemmed-In Hollow was a favorite haunt of visiting Indians—Osage, Quapaw, and others. They would come here to hunt and fish and to relax among the limestone bluffs and Ozark forest.

According to legend, the Indians suddenly stopped coming to Hemmed-In Hollow around the mid-1860s. Some claim it was because an increasing number of white settlers were moving into the area, but the natives tell a different story.

In 1863, something happened at Hemmed-In Hollow that frightened the Indians away. According to historian Mark Rocineaux, an Osage hunting party stopped at Hemmed-In Hollow to spend a few days relaxing, drying meat, and tanning deer hides. Early on the morning of the second day, one of the Indians awoke and walked the short distance from the campground to the river to fill a container with water. As he squatted on a gravel bar, he was suddenly startled by the appearance of a strange figure rising up out of the middle of the stream.

The Indian dropped the container and fell back to look upon a monstrosity—a creature that was half man and half fish—that stood in the middle of the stream and regarded him with a menacing glare.

When the creature began approaching the bank, the Indian turned and fled back toward the campground to warn his companions. After listening to the account of the encounter with the river creature, the Osage leaders decided it would be prudent to pack up and move back toward the north. They never returned to Hemmed-In Hollow again.

During the 1880s, white settlers began moving into the region. They felled trees, notched and hewed logs, and constructed cabins, barns, cribs, and smokehouses. Here and there, communities sprang up, and Hemmed-In Hollow became a favorite location for short outings, vacations, picnics, family reunions, revivals, and campouts.

One Saturday afternoon during the month of July in 1887, two families—the Hortons and the McAlisters—decided to take a break from the farm chores and travel the short distance from their homes to Hemmed-In Hollow. Here they planned to relax, have a picnic, and do a bit of fishing before returning to their homes.

Only minutes after the families arrived at Hemmed-In Hollow in horse-drawn wagons, several children bounded away and dashed down to the river to play in the water. As the parents spread blankets and set out food that was prepared earlier, the carefree youngsters splashed and frolicked in the waters of the calmly flowing Buffalo River.

The mothers were preparing to summon their children for lunch when a scream echoed throughout the river valley, one immediately accompanied by others, all coming from the children playing in the stream.

The parents ran toward the Buffalo River only to be met by the children fleeing toward the campground. When the children finally calmed down, they haltingly told of a strange creature, a monster that rose out of the middle of the river and glared at them. The thing, they said, was taller than a full-grown man, had arms and legs, but possessed the torso and facial features of a catfish!

After staring at the terror-stricken children for a moment, the creature began to advance toward them, at which point the youngsters turned and fled toward the safety of their parents. When the parents finally ventured down to the river to investigate, they found nothing.

The story of the brief encounter with the Buffalo River monster spread throughout the region. Others who had been silent until then, came forth and told of similar experiences with a strange fish-like being they also encountered at Hemmed-In Hollow. Before long, visits to the once-popular location declined significantly. Between the 1880s and the 1930s, most area residents avoided the area altogether.

During the 1940s, access to a variety of locations along the Buffalo River was increased via new and well-maintained roads. Before long, Hemmed-In

Hollow again became a favored destination for picnickers, campers, and hikers from as far away as Little Rock and Fayetteville and even Springfield, Missouri.

This new generation of vacationers and picnickers arrived at Hemmed-In Hollow with no knowledge whatsoever of the old Osage tales of the creature that supposedly lurked here or of the monster that frightened early settlers. With carefree and spirited abandon, the newcomers reveled in this glorious Ozark setting, hiked the trails, swam and fished in the Buffalo River, and took photographs of the picturesque Ozark settings.

Nothing particularly noteworthy relative to what was now being called the Buffalo River Monster occurred until 1947, when two brothers, Oscar and Curtis Williams, fourteen and eleven years old respectively, were playing in the stream at Hemmed-In Hollow. After about two hours of swimming and splashing around in the stream, the two boys made their way to the bank and lay down to rest before returning to the campground and their parents. After a few minutes, they fell asleep.

Suddenly, Oscar and Curtis were awakened by a commotion in the river. Roused from their slumber, the two boys sat up and stared out into the stream in search of the source of the disturbance. There, approximately thirty yards away and hip-deep in the water, was a strange creature neither had ever seen before. Thrashing about, the monster growled and screamed, according to a later statement from Curtis Williams. It appeared to be frustrated, he said. After observing the thing for about fifteen minutes, the brothers ran back toward the campground and excitedly informed their parents of what they had seen. When they returned to the stream, the creature was gone.

Little was heard or seen of the Buffalo River Monster until 1966. During the summer of that year, a group of students from the University of Arkansas at Fayetteville traveled to Hemmed-In Hollow for a weekend of partying and drinking beer.

On the evening of the day of arrival, two coeds, Lynn Brighton and Laura Glasscock, grew tired of the beer-guzzling and loud conversation of their peers and, seeking some peace and solitude, walked down to the Buffalo River where they reclined on the gravel bar next to the stream.

As they discussed the disgusting behavior of their respective dates, the two young women were suddenly surprised by the appearance of an odd shape out in the middle of the stream. At first, they thought it was a member of their party, but as the form approached the shoreline where they were sitting, they could see that it was monstrous—a half-man and half-catfish shape they later described as "utterly grotesque." Screaming, they leaped to their feet and fled back to the party, trying desperately to describe what they had seen.

On hearing of the experience, several of the more adventurous males ventured down to the riverbank but could detect no evidence of a monster. One of the men, Tom Rushing, waded into the water almost up to his waist, turned around to face the group standing on the shore, smiled, and said there was nothing to worry about.

A moment later, the water around Rushing swirled and, amid the screams of terror from those standing on the shore, a figure materialized behind him. Turning and regarding the horrifying specter of the Buffalo River Monster, Rushing attempted to hasten to shore only to be grabbed by the creature. His companions, standing only a few yards away, watched as the grotesque thing seized Rushing in pincer-like claws, hoisted him high above its head, and after shaking him as a cat would shake a mouse, tossed him toward the bank.

Rushing landed, skidded on the cobbled shoreline, dazed and abraded. Later, when his injuries were inspected, it was discovered he also suffered several deep cuts where the creature had grabbed him in its powerful grip.

In 1980, the level of the Buffalo was down somewhat because of a severe drought that had struck the region. While several families cooked and picnicked near Hemmed-In Hollow, some youngsters, ranging in age from five to eleven years of age wandered down to the river and began skipping stones. All went well for about an hour when suddenly, a bizarre shape walked out of the nearby forest and approached the children. Later when questioned by the sheriff, the youngsters all agreed the frightening intruder looked like it was half-man and half-fish. Though it was horrid in appearance, it did not appear to wish to harm anyone, only to see what was going on.

When the children raced back to the campground and informed their parents of what had transpired, one of the adults, Robert Blankenship grabbed a thick branch and ran down to the river. Just as he arrived, he related later, he saw the form of something wading in the river about fifty yards downstream. "It was about the size of man," said Blankenship, "but it looked for all the world like a huge catfish with legs and arms." Blankenship watched the creature for several minutes until it ducked into the shallow water and swam away.

Today, Hemmed-In Hollow remains a popular destination with people seeking solace and refuge from the big cities. In fact, more people than ever are visiting this beautiful Ozark location for camping, picnicking, and hiking. Sightings of the Buffalo River Monster have diminished considerably, and most visitors return home with nothing but pleasant and positive experiences of this serene Ozark setting.

Once in a while, however, a camper leaves Hemmed-In Hollow, vowing never to return because of what he or she has seen. Though most are reluctant to discuss their experiences, several have related to friends that they saw something they will never forget—a frightening, unspeakable monster that looked to be half man and half fish, rising from the waters of the Buffalo River.

Printed in the USA
CPSIA information can be obtained
at www.ICGtesting.com
LVHW041537210424
778013LV00028B/568

9 781930 584112